JILLEEN
DOLBEARE

Splintered Fate

VINCI
BOOKS

By Jilleen Dolbeare

Splintered Magic

Vinci Books

vinci-books.com

Published by Vinci Books Ltd in 2025

1

FSC
www.fsc.org

MIX
Paper | Supporting
responsible forestry
FSC® C018072

Printed and bound in Great Britain by Clays Ltd, Elcograf S.p.A.

Chapter One

The centaurs marched us by force down the hill towards a white castle gleaming in the sun. I dripped with sweat and shook with exhaustion and terror. Their weapons, mainly crossbows and spears, remained trained on the three of us. I'd always assumed centaurs would be mainly male, but these were all female. They were tall—their heads were probably two feet above mine—not that I was taller than average. I was surprised that their faces and what I could see of their torsos were remarkably human looking except for their ears, which were elongated and pointy—even sharper than the Lord of the Rings elves I kept waiting to see.

They wore intricately embossed, bright silver armor on their human torsos and their horse bodies as well. I wanted to take a closer look, but the fierce-looking leader kept us moving, and since I'd been poked once with a very sharp spear, I took it seriously—I wasn't sure if I should be regularly afraid or over the top terrified. I think I was a bit shocked that I'd accidentally realm walked us to Faerie. Who knew I had that kind of juice?

"What is that place?" I asked Mr. Mittens, who trotted along silently in front of me in his fearsome four-hundred-pound Splintercat form. The gleaming white castle looked gigantic in the light of the foreign sun.

It is the castle of the High King, he answered into my mind.

"The High King?" I trailed off when I stumbled and got poked again with the spear of the centaur apparently assigned to me. "Dammit." I yelled back at her, but she only poked me again.

"What do you think he'll do to us?" I whispered this time.

Mr. Mittens's mind voice was strained. *I do not know.*

"Do you think he knows my great-grandfather?" I continued to press.

Yes. He does.

That sent my mind on a tumble. I didn't know what to think about it. Did that mean they were friends? Enemies? Frenemies? I shivered. Megan bumped me from behind.

"Sorry," she mumbled.

I'd have reached back to comfort her, but I didn't dare. I already had three holes in me and didn't want a fourth. Who knew what kind of germs those wicked-looking spears had? At least they'd put away the crossbows. I could imagine the damage one of those would do if they went off accidentally—or on purpose. I shivered.

"What do they want with us?" Megan gasped behind me. We were marching along a well-used road and going a little faster than we were used to walking. It was hard on top of our general exhaustion.

"I don't know. Mr. Mittens said we are going to the castle of the High King."

2

Mr. Mittens didn't add anything.

Megan gave an exasperated sigh but didn't ask any more questions. She was probably also tired of getting poked and deep in her own set of worries. Mainly, what had she gotten into when she'd agreed to come to Oregon to help me?

I was worried for us, but part of my mind also worried about Sofia running loose in Faerie. What kind of mischief could she get up to, and what would it mean for us? I should have had Mr. Mittens eat her when we arrived, but I'd been too surprised, and a bit muddle headed from the air and the magic. Also, I wondered if Gabe was OK? I'd left him with the rest of the coven, unconscious and unable to take care of himself. Hopefully, Brightfeather, Goch, Noah, Luke, and the rest of the werewolves had helped him escape safely. I could only hope. Despair weighed me down, and my shoulders hunched.

With nothing much to do but wallow and walk, I studied the scenery and the back of the two centaurs in front of us. Faerie was lush and beautiful. The sun was warm, but not overpowering, and the green of the surrounding forests and grasses were intense. The breeze smelled of flowers and the sweetness of spring. In contrast, the centaur females were fierce and hard looking. They wore elaborate helmets that caught the light. The helmets looked more decorative than useful, since they left their ears free and didn't cover their cheeks or nose. The shine from the silver armor gleamed so much you could see them from space if Faerie had satellites. I had to blink and look away often to avoid blinding myself. The helmets and armor must be some kind of ceremonial wear I couldn't imagine sneaking up on an enemy in all that bling.

The centaurs in front of us also had long elaborate

braids under the helmets that swept down their backs like a horse's mane. Maybe that was the effect they were after, or maybe their hair actually did go down their backs like a horse's mane. The braids seemed secured to the armor, or their flesh, since the hair didn't sway back and forth as they walked. I wasn't close enough to see if the hair was attached to their backs or just secured to the armor.

Huh. If we weren't in terrible danger, I'd love to spend time studying these creatures. They were strange but majestic.

I stumbled again and got another poke for it. I took it back. They were not majestic, sadistic, maybe. I threw an angry glare at my poker but knew better than to swear at her again. She didn't even look at me. Hell, I didn't even know if we spoke the same language, or if they could even speak at all. We'd climbed a hill and were now looking down at the trail around the lake. It was lovely, well-maintained, and park-like. The trail seemed groomed, and the grass trimmed to an even length. The leader turned and headed down the hill.

They stopped us once and let us drink from the pristine waters of the lake. I tried not to worry about parasites or bacteria or anything else; I was too thirsty. Hopefully, being from a different world would protect us from the local infections. I looked through the crystal-clear water at the gem like rocks underneath the surface. A brightly colored fish sparkled in the depths. I might have smiled—I don't know for sure; I was too tired and scared—but the beauty around me kept surprising and delighting me regardless of the dangers. I scooped up water in my hands and drank what felt like a gallon. My thirst eased, I rinsed off the blood spots on my skin from getting poked, threw water in my face, and that was it. Time was up. The centaurs sped up and kept us marching until we reached the castle.

I took back my thought that this place *wasn't* like *The Lord of the Rings*. The architecture of the castle would fit right in. Lofty, sweeping, and ethereal, the intricate carving and design of the place was CGI worthy. It was so beautiful, and I yearned to be part of it. I couldn't even put into words the incredible spectacle it was. My mind wasn't clever enough to even create a place like this in a dream. It *was* Rivendell. Had Tolkien been here? Probably. Hope a centaur poked him. That's what he deserved for crushing my dreams about elves. I was still ticked that my grandfather hadn't looked like Legolas. Maybe I should be mad at Peter Jackson. *Hmmm.*

The walls were gleaming white like sun-bleached bone. I wanted to touch them, see what they were made of, but the centaurs kept us moving through the courtyard without pause. They finally stopped before a large, intricately carved door. It was covered with fantastical beasts and scenes that I didn't recognize—probably because I was on an unfamiliar world. Just as the doors began to open, I thought I caught a carving of some unicorns—the nasty bastards—but I wasn't allowed the time to study if that were true. On the other side of the door were more guards, two-footed this time, still in fancy shiny armor. They took over our care and marched us into the interior of the castle. At least we'd slowed down a little.

I looked at Megan. She looked at me. Fear reflected in her eyes, as I'm sure it did in mine. Mr. Mittens slowly shrank until he walked by us in his Ragdoll form, his glowing fur more noticeable on this magic rich planet. I wondered if that was emotion or design on his part. He'd been reserved since we'd been captured, and this made him seem scared. I'd *never* seen my cat afraid for himself before.

We were eventually ushered into a massive chamber. The ceilings were almost too high to be seen, and it was easily as spacious as an indoor professional sports arena. I looked around. People and unfamiliar creatures, wearing intricate robes in riotous colors and lush fabrics, milled around. The guards forced us forward. I stumbled and almost fell, but Megan grabbed my arm.

At the far end of the massive room, up on a dais, a robed and crowned figure sat. The High King, I assumed. I gulped. Megan slid her hand down my arm and grabbed my hand. Mr. Mittens's solid warmth pressed against my legs. He pressed on me so hard, I almost tripped again. We walked forward in our tight group, touching each other for comfort.

Finally, they stopped us and forced us to kneel before the dais. I trembled, as did Megan beside me. Mr. Mittens seemed smaller than his usual self, but when the king addressed him, he walked forward boldly, head and tail raised. I couldn't understand the king's words, and I felt a momentary panic, but then I realized his voice echoed in my mind and I could understand the meaning. I looked around. Did magic act like a universal translator here? I checked the ceiling. Was the room a universal translator? I didn't see anything that proved it *wasn't*.

"Xrsrphn, did we not banish you from this realm?" The King's voice was thunderous.

I thought I saw Mr. Mittens flinch. *Yes, sire.*

That was the reason he was so reluctant and afraid. Now that I knew he'd been banished, I was afraid for him. Would they take him away from me? Was this how they found us so quickly?

"Why are you here?" The king truly sounded as if he was curious. He didn't sound angry or accusatory. I felt a surge of relief.

I was brought here accidentally by my charge. His tail flicked at the tip, his anxiety palpable to me but probably not to others.

The King's gaze landed on us. He dismissed Megan, and the full weight of it landed on me.

"You are the progeny of my Pendragon?" he asked.

Was this a trick question? If he asked, he had to already know. He knew my cat and the terms of his banishment. Mr. Mittens had told me he was under a geas to protect my grandfather's progeny. So, that identified me immediately.

What was a Pendragon? I wasn't sure what that title meant here. I remembered that King Arthur's dad was Uther Pendragon. Did that make my grandfather a prince here? Wow, if that were true.

"Y-y-yes?" I stammered, uncertainly. I wondered if my single word was translated into the king's head as his were in mine.

He looked me up and down. Not the typical look you got from a man checking you out but an assessing look. And I didn't make the cut. I felt a teensy bit annoyed at that. Sure, I was a mess now, but I didn't think I was a total hag.

"Interesting."

I guess that answered my question about the universal translator.

His gaze flicked to a servant standing nearby. The servant hurried over. The king issued a command I couldn't hear, and the servant scurried off to fulfill it. I shifted my weight from foot to foot in nervous anticipation.

"What have you brought with you to my Kingdom?" he finally addressed me again.

7

I wasn't sure what he meant, and my face must have shown that because his gaze flicked to Megan and back.

"This is my friend, Megan," I said, not knowing what else he wanted.

"This is a *human?*" he asked, stumbling over the word "human" slightly.

"Yes, we both are," I added. Then I realized that might not be true. I wondered how much of me was actually human. By birth, I'd say I was an eighth Fae, seven-eighths human, but I had all of this power. I didn't really know what would show on a DNA test. Did Fae genes overwrite human ones? It was something I would only investigate in a private lab—if I owned one—once we were home.

He didn't answer for a moment, staring at us both. He looked remarkably similar to a human. Humanoid, for sure. Two arms, two legs, both races appeared similar in height. It was hard to tell since he was seated above us, but I'd put him at around six feet tall. He had long golden hair that was swept back. He did have slightly pointed ears, but I'd seen humans with equally pointed ears, so he could pass if he dressed like a modern human.

He was richly dressed in a long golden gown that was belted with a soft cord. Over that, he wore a large robe type garment that was made of some kind of fur. It was thick, white, and looked incredibly soft. He stood and walked down the three steps from his throne to us. Our guards straightened and became even more alert. They moved their weapons closer to us until the king waved them back. I breathed a sigh of relief. He came close enough to sniff us. Which he did. That startled me the most. I recoiled slightly, not enough to anger him, but enough he looked at me with surprise.

"You smell Fae," he said to me.

He sniffed Megan again, and his lip curled. He backed away. Just then, the servant that he'd sent came jogging back into the throne room. He cast about, looking for the king. When he spotted him, he hurried over.

"Sire, he is on his way." He then bowed and scraped his way back to where he'd stood originally.

The king glanced at us one more time and returned to his throne. He waved a dismissive hand, and we were guided back to a spot along the wall. Two guards remained, weapons trained on us, but we were forgotten for the moment.

People came and went, meeting with the king, but we were so absorbed watching and trying to figure out the local culture that we missed much of what the king was doing. I wondered what would happen to us, what the king would do to us when he remembered we were here.

It felt like hours that we stood there. If we slumped or looked like we would do more than shuffle our feet, the guards would force us back to attention. It was exhausting. I didn't even know I could get more tired, since I was exhausted *before* the centaurs had captured us. On top of it, my feet hurt and my back ached. I could tell that Megan was uncomfortable and tired as well. Even Mr. Mittens drooped a little. We'd been through a battle, a transport to another world, and a forced march over miles of varied terrain. We were too tired for this standing at attention crap.

Just before I burst into tears of exhaustion and frustration, the court stilled, and all the background noise stopped. I'd thought it was quiet considering all the people packed into this room before, but the deafening silence that followed proved me wrong. All eyes were drawn to the door we'd walked through initially. The door swung open, and a massive red-headed man walked in.

9

He was built like a brick—tall, solid, and menacing. His presence drew everyone's gaze like a moth to a flame. Even mine. He was in a shiny suit of linked mail, covered with hard leather armor. He had an ax strapped to his broad leather belt, along with a sword. It was a wonder he didn't clank when he walked or lose his drawers. I tittered. I'd had the same thought the first time I'd seen him. No way a *non*-magical belt was holding up all that metal. But since he wasn't walking bare-assed into the throne room, he must have a secret to keeping his pants up.

The crowd parted before him. My great-grandfather did not stop or slow until he stood before the throne.

He bowed his head respectfully but didn't kneel. I thought that was telling.

"Sire," he stated. "How may I serve you?" His voice boomed to every corner of the room. The crowd seemed to hold its breath and wait to see what would happen. Including me.

The king looked at my grandfather fondly. "I believe I have something of yours, my dear Pendragon," he stated and gestured to the guards. They grabbed Megan and me by our arms and roughly dragged us back to the throne. Mr. Mittens trailed in our wake. If they knew that Mr. Mittens was much scarier than us, they'd have rethought that move and grabbed him instead.

My grandfather frowned at me. Then looked away dismissively. My heart sank.

"Thank you, sire. I have no idea how this came to be. I'm very sorry to have troubled you," he said.

"No bother. My Scáthanna picked them up while training—once they felt the portal open and the presence of the cat. They needed the practice responding quickly to threats." Ah, that must be what the female centaurs were called. The king's tone was flippant, not bothered, and I sagged with relief on the inside. Maybe we weren't a big deal, and we'd be allowed to leave. I looked down at Mr. Mittens; he had sunk even closer to the ground and looked completely miserable.

This time, my grandfather gave a deep bow. "I am honored that you would watch over them, sire. I'll remove them from your gracious care."

"We will speak later." The king waved him and us away.

My grandfather froze briefly, then gestured at us. I grabbed Megan's hand and followed him closely—Mr. Mittens in tow. I could feel the concentrated worry and rage rolling off my grandfather's back as he walked stiffly in front of us and out the doors of the throne room. I'd really done it now. Feeling like a naughty child being picked up from school by an angry parent, I marched behind him. I was forty-two—way too old for this crap.

Chapter Two

We entered a room in the High King's castle. It was plain
white like the rest of the building but contained nothing
except an elaborate circle emblazoned on the floor and us. I
reached a hand out to the wall; I still wanted to know what
the material the palace was made of. The wall felt smooth
and cool to the touch, like marble, but it wasn't marble. I
frowned. I wasn't even sure if it was stone, bone, or a super
hard wood. My grandfather waved for us to move inside the
circle. We did. The circle was of a silvery metal with runes
and hieroglyphs embedded in it. I wanted to lean down and
touch it too, but I didn't have time. He closed his eyes briefly
and mumbled something. A flash surrounded us. I blinked the
light from my eyes and looked around. We were in a new but
similar room, except the stone walls were now a silvery grey,
rather than the white of the high king's palace. My grandfather strode forward, opened the door, and walked boldly
down a corridor. We followed, not knowing what else to do.

He ushered us into a large room with a huge fireplace

and comfortable seating. One wall was floor to ceiling book-shelves complete with a rolling ladder, just like an old-fash-ioned library on Earth. There was also a heavy wooden table—carved and ornate. I'd call this a library or at least a private den or study if we were home. Megan was squeezing my hand painfully, probably as terrified as I was. At least we'd not been executed or accused of anything—yet. However, my grandfather was still holding back his anger, if his high color and flashing eyes were any indication.

"What are you doing here?" His voice was quiet, firm, and demanding all at once.

I looked at Megan; she looked at me. Mr. Mittens was standing extra quietly behind me, out of range, I assumed.

I cleared my throat. "Well, it wasn't intentional." I scuffed my feet, glancing up at him briefly before continu-ing. "Umm, we were fighting the witches. I think we were even coming out on top, but I panicked and accidentally brought us to Faerie. Now, I have no magic," I added as an afterthought. I threw up my hands.

"Hmpf," he said. That startled me. Did Mr. Mittens get that particular response from my great-grandfather or vice versa? Something to think about.

He was quiet, tension radiating from him. He turned his back to us and faced the fire. The fireplace was easily as tall as my grandfather and wider than my large sofa at home. You could roast a whole cow in it, if Faerie had cows—I didn't know. After a moment, he moved away, pulled out his ax and sword, and laid them on the heavy wooden table. He stretched his back. I was right, all that metal had to be uncomfortable. He loosened his wide, heavy sword belt and added it to the pile, along with the hard leather armor and shiny mail. Underneath, he wore a simple black high-necked tunic and pants.

Then he sat in a comfortable looking chair by the fire.

"Sit," he commanded.

We chose seats away from him on the opposite side of the fireplace and sat—none of us daring to disobey. He sighed loudly.

"You don't know what kind of position you have placed me in," he began, wearily.

I must have made a noise because he threw me a glance that would have shut up much scarier people than me. I shut up.

"The High King did me a favor. I will owe him."

I felt terrible. I had no idea what the favor would entail, but I hated anyone feeling like they had to do anything for me. I had some slight control issues.

"You do not understand our culture. I know that, and I didn't expect for you to come here until you were fully trained and cognizant of our ways."

That seemed more like he was talking to himself. But I hadn't *intended* for us to come here either.

"This is a dilemma. I'll have to present you formally at court. There will be other...repercussions. I might be able to delay until your magic regenerates. We'll see. I'm hoping the king forgets, but this was unusual enough, I'm afraid he will not."

I gulped. I had no idea what that meant or what it would mean for us, but my grandfather's worry terrified me.

His gaze swung to Mr. Mittens, who visibly flinched. "You have my permission to use your shifting magic in my presence during your time here."

Mr. Mittens looked relieved, like he was waiting for a

blow, and it didn't come. He bowed his head and shifted back into the Fae form he'd shown us briefly when we landed in Faerie.

"Thank you, my lord," he said and gave a slight bow.

It was disconcerting to see my cat in this form. I knew he was a cat or cat adjacent, and seeing him with two arms and two legs threw me. His eyes stayed the same though; that was comforting. I noticed his feet were still bare and grinned to myself. He'd probably still sleep in the middle of the bed and jump in boxes. What had he done to anger the Fae?

"I must think on this," my grandfather said after a long pause. He pulled on a rope dangling near his chair, summoning a servant.

"Take them to the guest quarters, and send some food as well."

The servant bowed and gestured for us to follow.

Before I was sent to my bed, I turned and faced him. "What is a Pendragon?" I was curious, and I felt I must commit a small defiance.

He glanced at me, then away. "I'm the High King's Commander." Then he dismissed me with a wave of his hand.

Commander? Did that mean he was like a general or something? I had so many questions.

The servant led us through the keep. We wound our way through corridors and up multiple types of stairs. I was profoundly lost after the second spiral staircase. The castle —that was the only word for it—was mostly grey stone with dark wooden accents in the doors and wainscoting lining the corridors in some places. Someone had made an effort to decorate the corridors and make the castle feel homey with portraits, landscapes and occasional huge vases with flowering plants and vines at regular intervals. I tried to look at everything once I realized I'd never find my way back without a guide.

Finally, we stopped before a door; the servant opened it and gestured for Mr. Mittens to enter. He walked in, gave a slight bow to us, and shut the door. The servant dropped Megan off at the next door, and she looked at me nervously before entering. I told her I'd check on her. The next room was for me.

I didn't know what to expect from a Faerie dwelling. Particularly one in a castle. So far, my grandfather's residence seemed like a normal Earth castle, though lacking electricity. The window coverings were open, and light streamed in. The room was large, and the focus was on an enormous bed with rich furs and forest green coverings. I sighed. I wanted to sink into it and forget everything, but I was dirty, sticky, and sore. The rest of the room could qualify as a type of medieval hotel. There was a large wooden table with chairs, a wardrobe, and a few comfortable chairs covered with colorful tapestry type fabric near the window with another small table and a lamp. That area would make a comfortable reading nook. The lamp had oil and a wick, I discovered, as did the lamps on the bedside table. I didn't see a way to light them, and since my magic was gone, I couldn't use my fire magic either. I shrugged; I'd worry about it when it got dark. For all I knew, there was a servant in charge of lamps.

I looked around for a bathroom; there was another door in addition to the one we came through. I opened it. There was a chamber that fit the bill. A large coppery colored tub dominated the room, and I wondered if there was such a thing as hot water on this strange world. Shouldn't anything be possible with magic?

The tub did have a faucet and handles, not much different than in my home. I turned on the tap and found hot water. A grateful sigh escaped me. I plugged the tub and let it fill. On the outside wall, near a window, was a doorless closet—a garderobe. I walked over and examined it. It was basically an ornate wooden seat with a hole. It didn't smell, so wherever the waste went, it was far away. I shuddered. But I used it quickly. I was full to bursting. If I hadn't been dehydrated, I'd have never made it through the ordeal at court. There was a cabinet with towels and soaps, so I stripped off my filthy and torn garments and climbed into the tub. The warmth was glorious, and I sank under the water until nothing was exposed. *Great tubs are deep enough for a thorough soak,* I thought as the warmth melted the ache from my back muscles and sore feet.

Once the water started to get cold, I hurriedly lathered and rinsed. I climbed out, dried, and wrapped myself in a towel. My clothes were toast, too filthy and tattered to put back on. I fumbled around the room, searching for something else to wear. I found the wardrobe full of clothing and pulled a deep blue robe out that glided against my skin like silk. It took a moment to figure out the strange multitude of fastenings. The robe smelled like a spring morning, and I sniffed it and let it fall back in place. There were soft little slippers of some kind of leather. They also went on like silk and fit like a glove. I was confused. How did anyone know my size?

I hurried down to Megan's room, assuming she would just be getting out of the bath the same as me. I knocked. The door was hard, wooden, and heavy, and it hurt my knuckles. I shrugged, assuming that made for good security. I couldn't hear her, so I tried the handle. I hadn't really examined my door for a lock, and apparently neither had Megan, because I walked through without a problem.

"Megan?" I said in a normal voice.

There was a shriek from behind a closed door.

"It's just me!" I yelled louder.

"I'm in the bathroom; give me a minute."

I looked around her room, which was almost exactly the same as mine. The only difference was that instead of dark green, the bedding and furniture were in shades of dark purple.

I sat on the bed and waited a few minutes. "Do you have clean clothes, or do you want me to hand you some?" I asked when I grew bored.

"I'm good," she answered. A few seconds later, she entered the bedroom.

"You have good taste," I remarked when she walked out in the identical robe to the one I was wearing. She looked at me, then we both burst into laughter.

"They must buy guest clothing in bulk," Megan said.

"Let's see!" I stood and opened her wardrobe. Sure enough, they both had the same garments within.

"I wonder how sizes work here?" I said.

"Magic?" she quipped. After a moment, she continued, "Hmmm, I think they're all just a 'one size fits all' thing." She pulled another robe out of the wardrobe. "See, these ties and things are adjustable."

I shrugged. I hadn't paid much attention when I'd put mine on, but it made sense and explained the multitude of ties and fasteners on each garment.

"Smart."

She nodded.

"When do you think they're sending up that food? I'm starving."

"Yeah, me too," I agreed.

"Should we go look or wait?" She stood and looked around the room. "Think there's one of those rope pull thingies around?"

There wasn't, or at least not one we could see.

"I think we should check on Mr. Mittens first. He's spent time here; he might know how things work. Plus, I'm sure I'll never find my way back if we go further than our three rooms."

She nodded, and we headed to his door. I wasn't sure what we'd see if we walked in, so I knocked again. There wasn't an answer. Did he go back to his natural form or was he in the bath? Did magical shapeshifting cats bathe when they weren't in cat form? Huh.

"Do you think he's having a bath?" Megan echoed my thought.

"I really don't know."

Come in, your conversation is draining, a tired voice said in my mind.

We looked at each other and entered the room. It was another room identical to ours, only in shades of blue. Mr. Mittens was in his Splintercat form, sprawled in the middle of the bed. At least that was a normal sight. His huge round head with his long killer teeth swung towards us.

Are you not tired? he asked.

"Yeah, exhausted, but we're starved. How do you get food brought up?" Megan asked.

He gave his usual exasperated cat sigh. *You pull the cord. It notifies the serving quarters, and someone will come.*

"Where is it? We looked all over," I asked.

He pulled himself up into a standing position and stepped off the bed. He walked over to the wardrobe and glanced behind it. *It is there, close to the wardrobe corner, out of sight. Now, shouldn't you go eat and rest? I have a feeling tomorrow will be even more draining.*

Concerned, I asked. "Did you eat, Mr. Mittens?"

No.

"Do you want to eat with us?" I asked.

I wish to rest. He hopped back up on the bed, found a spot, and plopped down.

We looked at each other, both of us frowning thoughtfully.

"Come on," I said to Megan, "we better go so we can all rest."

We proceeded back to Megan's room. "Stay with me?" she asked.

I shrugged. I was feeling odd here, too. I wished my cat was with me, but here he could be more of a what?...entity? person? than he could on Earth. Plus, he didn't have to protect me in my grandfather's house. I guess he deserved to be off duty for a time.

I didn't want to be alone. So, I walked in. Megan pulled the silken rope we located just where Mr. Mittens had indicated.

When the food came, it was beautifully exotic to look at —colorful and fanciful shapes and interesting arrangements. I wasn't sure what was animal, vegetable, or mineral. Megan and I looked at each other.

"Is it safe for us to eat?" she said, voicing what I was thinking.

"I guess, I mean people have talked about going to Faerie before, and they always say the food is great." I frowned at the beautiful dishes and the food items upon them.

"Yeah, but then they tell you not to partake of any food or drink, or you're trapped here forever."

"Are you sure that's for Faerie or Hades?" I asked, not sure.

"I'm sure it's for both," she said, a sarcastic twist to her words. That meant she didn't have a clue.

"Really? Because you have degrees in mythology and folklore?" I threw out.

"Yup! So, we should send this back. People can go weeks without food." She frowned. "I think."

I picked up a flower. That's the only way I could describe it. It was purple and gold. It was obviously something edible, but it was in the shape of a delicate flower. I wasn't sure how to hold it, it looked too dainty to just pick up, but it held together as I examined it. Megan was pacing, still debating if she should eat the food. My head swam, and I didn't think that my grandfather would do anything to put me at risk. Gruff as he was, he seemed dutiful or at least concerned. I mean the Fae had to care for their own children just as well we cared for ours, right? Otherwise, their civilization would collapse.

I took a bite. It crunched at first, but then sent a shiver of delight through me. The taste was simultaneously sweet and savory, if that was possible. And I mean beyond the usual salt and sugar delight of a good dessert. I moaned.

Megan whipped around, still talking about whether or not we should eat.

"What are you doing?" she screeched then slapped the rest out of my hand. It shattered on the stone floor.

"Why did you do that?" I asked, staring at the broken flower.

"We decided we couldn't eat or drink while we're here."

"*We* did not decide that. *You did.* I'm hungry, and it's good. Like really good," I said and picked up another exotic looking food item.

I took a bite before she could grab it away from me. Another culinary delight. Sunshine exploded in my mouth; I tasted summer and happiness. I figured this was a fruit of some kind. It vaguely reminded me of a peach. Sort of a firm but gentle flesh that gave away to my teeth and filled my mouth with juicy delight. Yet, it was so much more than a peach from my world. I'd never be the same again. Like the saturation of color and the richness of the air, even the food was superior to Earth. I was beginning to understand why people were cautioned not to eat when in Faerie. Not because the food was bad, but because you would never be satisfied with Earth food again.

I finished the fruit—whatever it was—and looked at Megan. She glared at me.

"Just eat. You'll never be satisfied with food again, but it's wonderful, and we need to keep our strength up."

She gave a disgusted snort at me and picked up another fruit similar to what I'd just eaten. I watched her as she bit into it. Ecstasy spread across her face when the flavors hit her.

"Damn," was all she said when she finished. She stared at the other food. "That was better than sex. No, better than chocolate." She grabbed another flower. Only this one was red and orange. She bit into it and groaned. She offered me half, and I ate it as well. It was similar to the last one but sweeter.

We both looked at the next unidentifiable food design. It looked more solid than the flowers, or even the delicate fruits. Maybe it was meat of some kind. I sniffed it. It smelled spicy and savory. I took an experimental bite. It had the mouth feel of meat, but the flavor was again unique. It was spicy smoky, and a tiny bit sweet, with an almost imperceptible gaminess that on earth you could find revolting but with the other flavors only accentuated the deliciousness. Plus, it melted in your mouth like good barbecue ribs. We ate everything. I even tasted the plates, just in case. They were not edible, unfortunately, because I'm sure they'd taste divine as well.

"OK, food is fabulous here," Megan said with a satisfied sigh.

"Yes, oh yes, better than anything I've ever had!" I licked my fingers.

"Even Gabe?" Megan said slyly.

"I don't know, I haven't had him yet," I said snippily. Talking about him immediately put me in a bad mood. I felt horribly guilty that I'd left him alone and unconscious in the woods with a coven of evil witches.

"Sorry, I shouldn't have brought him up," Megan replied. "That was dumb."

I shook my head. "I feel helpless. All I can do is hope the werewolves retrieved him, and he's safe. But I don't know. He must think I abandoned him."

"He'd never think that. You fought so hard."

"Yeah, but he didn't see it. All he saw when he woke up was that I wasn't there."

"Well, at least Sofia wasn't either," she said.

"Yeah, that's one consolation. I hope something in Faerie ate her."

Megan giggled. "Yes, that would be awesome."

"Most likely she's rediscovered her magic, refilled on all the free stuff floating around here, found allies, and is now back on earth destroying all that I own," I said, the weight of everything bowing my shoulders and dragging my mood all the way to the basement.

"Let's see if your grandpa can send us home in the morning. I'm sure he can," Megan tried to cheer me up.

"Yeah, maybe. I'm going to go to my room. I'm exhausted. Do you mind?" I asked, knowing she'd wanted me to stay.

"No, I'll be OK. The food helped," she replied.

"Night, Megan. Sorry I dragged you into all of this."

"You know I'd have found a way to be here with you no matter what. Don't worry about me."

That was why it was good to have a best friend.

Chapter Three

I woke up with a familiar warmth in the small of my back. I reached behind me to stroke Mr. Mittens's Ragdoll, cottony soft fur. I did that for a minute, before I sat up with a start. I was in a strange room with dark forest green curtains surrounding the bed. I blinked a few times before it all came back to me.

"Mr. Mittens! What are you doing in here?" I asked. I remembered he'd been set up in his own room.

I felt him stretch, and then he walked over my legs and sat down, facing me. I scratched his ears.

I am your protector. I came to watch over you while you slept, he said with a yawn, his teeth white and sharp.

"You can say you missed me. I missed you, too," I said.

Hmpf.

But he followed up his dismissive sound with a head butt and a demand for belly rubs and scritches.

I smiled. My cat made me happy. He was still the best companion I'd ever had. Definitely better than my ex, Evan —the man whore.

"What do you think will happen today? Do you think my grandfather will send us back?" I asked, hopefully.

It's more complicated than that. If we could have made it to your grandfather's home without running into any issues, he could have sent us back directly. Since we were captured by the king himself, we are at the mercy of the court. There is no easy way out of our dilemma. He leaned against me to groom a back leg.

"Well, shit. We can't stay here very long. I don't know what happened to the witches, or Gabe, or even the rest of our allies." My heart started to pound. I really didn't know what had happened, and now that I wasn't worried about my immediate safety, I was terrified that one of them was hurt, or worse, dead.

I'm sorry that my presence got us captured, he said.

"Is that why you were out of sorts yesterday?" I asked him, while scratching behind his ears.

He didn't answer, but his purr grew louder. I took that as a "Yes, I'm sorry."

"It wasn't your fault. I'm the one that dumped us here, I don't blame you."

There was a sharp knock on my door. Since Megan would just waltz in. I jumped, and my heart hammered. I knew it wasn't her. Mr. Mittens jumped down, and I leapt out of bed and grabbed the robe I'd discarded on the chair the night before. I hurriedly ran my fingers through my hair and wrapped the robe tightly around myself. I opened the door.

A servant stood there, dressed in what I was starting to recognize as my grandfather's livery—dark blue velvety tunic, tight leggings in black, and a stylized dragon emblazoned in silver on the breast.

I blinked.

"You are requested in the dining hall," he said with an imperious air.

Since I'd just awakened, I nodded and asked, "When?"

He looked me up and down. "After you are properly attired."

That didn't really give me a time limit, but I nodded and shut the door.

"Can you interpret that for me, please, Mr. Mittens?" I asked, as I hurriedly went into the bathroom to wash my face and do something with my hair.

They want you to wear something fit for court, would be my interpretation. I'll look inside your closet. Something should be waiting there for you.

I dried my face and smoothed the wild hairs that were shooting off in all directions. I had no straightener here, and no product, but the brush that was left behind did wonders to smooth my hair. I checked the wardrobe. Last night, it had been full of those one-size fits all robes. True, the material was dreamy, but they were more dressing gowns than something to wear at court. I didn't know how I'd missed anything else, but nonetheless I opened the closet door in hope.

"What?" I gasped in surprise. The closet was full of lovely garments—all things I'd consider fit for court. They looked fancy enough.

I picked out a gown—the perfect shade of blue for my eyes—and put it on. Like the magical closet, the second I pulled it over my head and the folds fell, the magical gown fastened itself, and fit itself to me perfectly. I glanced in the mirror. It was perfect in every way.

"This is amazing!" I crooned to my cat, who looked bored. I bet clothing wasn't anything he'd ever worried about. When he shifted, his spectacular spotted coat turned into a spotted robe in the Fae style.

After I'd looked at my reflection and maybe did a twirl, I told Mr. Mittens I was ready, and we headed to pick up Megan.

She too was excited about the magical clothing. She had to show me her closet before we left and exclaim over the ruby gown she had chosen. It was the perfect color for her skin tone and dark hair.

Together, we followed Mr. Mittens down corridor after twisting corridor and several stair cases until we were finally ushered into the dining hall. The room was large and pretty, a whole wall was replaced by floor-to-ceiling windows. The rest was covered in rich wood with plants hanging every-where. It was almost garden-like. The room was dominated by a long intricately carved table and chairs.

I expected a room full of people since we'd dressed up and the castle and dining room were so large, but it was just the three of us, my grandfather, and Dana, his mistress of magic. She frowned at me with her dead, shark eyes, and horsey face. The smile I planned to greet her with melted off my face. When my eyes flicked to my grandfather, I realized something was extremely wrong.

"What's wrong?" I asked. My voice breathy with distress.

My grandfather waved away my question with a hand. "We will discuss it after we eat. No sense being worried on an empty stomach."

That might work for him, but now my stomach was roiling with upset. What was so bad that everyone looked so glum? Had the king made a decision about me? Was there news from home? No, I dismissed that one. No one knew where we were or how to contact my grandfather. Was there a team of female centaurs outside to drag us to prison? Had Sofia regained her magic and brought a team of sorcerers against us? I shivered.

Food was brought out, and servants began piling items on our plates. I didn't have the energy to watch, or choose between selections, I just nodded when something was presented until there wasn't room left on my plate. The food was still beautiful and exotic, the flower things, fruit, and meat that I'd noticed before had been replaced by different versions of those items. Knowing I had to keep my strength up, I ate without tasting or thinking until I was full and pushed my plate away. I noticed Megan was basically doing the same. Mr. Mittens had transformed and was eating in his Fae form. He handled the eating utensils with graceful movements, so he must have spent significant time in this form at some point.

Maybe someday, he'd tell me his story. How had he ended up exiled and under a geas for my protection? He must have done something horrifying to the Fae. I couldn't imagine what. Then again, I had zero understanding of the local culture or customs. It could be easy to get myself exiled as well.

Once finished, Megan and I waited patiently for the dishes to be cleared and my grandfather to fill us in. When he could stall no longer, he stood and paced the large room, hands clasped behind his back. He was dressed in a beautifully embroidered blue tunic and dark trousers, his feet and legs encased in supple leather boots.

I watched each step, too nervous to look at his face and the worry etched on it.

"The king has sent a request this morning," his voice rumbled forth.

I looked up to view his face briefly. He was looking out

the long windows that framed one side of the dining hall. I only caught his profile. His jaw was clenched, and his eyes appeared pinched.

Not good.

I was going to ask, but before I got it out of my mouth, he continued, "He has requested your presence, officially, at court." He turned and faced me.

I met his eyes. "What does that mean exactly?"

He shook his head and sighed. "It is as your people would say, a mixed bag. It could just be a polite way of welcoming you as my granddaughter."

I felt a wave of relief.

But he wasn't done. "However, there are sinister implications that are more likely true."

My elation dimmed, and my stomach fell. This wasn't a good sign.

"In truth, we have been in the midst of a minor power struggle. He believes he can call on me for every minor fray." His voice rose, and his face reddened with fury. "I'm his Pendragon—the supreme commander. He can send his minor Drakes for that." He looked at our confused faces.

"Right." He shook his head, and his voice softened again. "That is not your concern. What is your concern is that he's found a way to control me—through you." He looked right at me.

My heart stopped, and then started and fluttered in my chest. Pure fear gripped me, and the blood drained from my head. I felt faint. "What do you m-mean?" I stuttered.

"If I'm right, he's going to propose one of two things. An alliance or..." He trailed off. "Something I don't want to do." He smiled at me.

"What does alliance mean?" I asked, my blood cold.

"Connecting our houses and political ties through marriage."

"Marriage?" For the life of me, I couldn't imagine how that concerned me. I was thinking that he wanted my single grandfather to marry his daughter or something and life flickered back into my soul. But then the implications finally hit me. If it was my grandfather whose marriage was imminent, my arrival wouldn't have changed anything. What made the difference was now my grandfather had a family member to bargain with. And that family member was me.

"You mean me?" my voice was a little shrill, and I cleared my throat.

"The king has been looking for a worthy consort. He requires a certain blood line, a strength in magic, and a political tie that would be worthy of a queen. I'm afraid you showed up in the middle of that search."

Damn my luck. I had enough problems on my own world, and I didn't give a *shit* about the High King's.

"No." I emphasized that by shaking my head. I might have stood up and even stepped back to escape.

My grandfather stiffened. He wasn't used to being disobeyed. I lowered my face so I wouldn't have to look at him. I sat back in my chair and scooted back up to the table. I could see Megan out of the corner of my eye. Her eyes were wide and fixed on my grandfather. Mr. Mittens melted from Fae into his Ragdoll form and jumped lightly into my lap. He was attempting to comfort me. I buried my fingers in his fur.

I put up my hands as though to deflect a blow. "I don't live here, and I don't intend to stay. Not to mention, I'm not for sale. I'm forty-two, infertile, and I have no intention of marrying anyone again." *Except I'd think about it if it were Gabe. Let him be alive.*

31

"We may not be given a choice." He started to pace again. "You don't know the history of this land or our culture."

I knew that. I didn't, but they were also about to oppose me on mine. I just wanted out.

"What does it matter? I'm not from here, and I intend to leave as soon as I can," I said stubbornly.

He stopped and shook his head. Then he turned to appeal to me. "Not too long ago, we were ruled not by one High King, but by four different courts. We divided ourselves into Summer, Winter, Spring, and Autumn Courts, and all the Fae aligned themselves with one or the other based upon their natures."

He started to pace again, agitated.

"But we fought for millennia over land and titles and who could claim which of the strongest of us. We were tearing our planet apart—both literally and figuratively. There was a final war shortly before I reached maturity, and the courts of old fell. We decided we should be one people under one ruler. We couldn't fight if we were one? Right? So, the strongest magic user took the throne. Someone who all would tremble before and not oppose."

"So, you're saying you cannot cross him in this?"

"I am not strong enough." He hung his head.

Dana had been silent through everything. I never thought of her as a friend, I knew she only helped me learn magic because my grandfather willed it, but she looked as though she wished to say something.

"What do you know, Dana?" I asked her. My grandfather's head whipped up, and he stared at her.

"You *could* oppose him, master," she replied not to me, but to him.

"Don't speak of this again; you know the conse-quences," he barked at her.

Her black shark eyes widened, but her lips thinned. Dutifully, she bowed her head. She didn't want to shut up. She knew something. "Yes, master."

My hands clenched. "Your High King didn't even like me. He acted as though he found me abhorrent," I said. It was true. He acted as though the fact I was from Earth made me lower than a bug in his eyes. "But today he wants me to marry him? Is he all there?"

"This has nothing to do with you, my granddaughter. This isn't personal past the parameters he requires of a bride. This is because of me." His eyes flitted to Dana, who remained demure, her eyes cast down. "What Dana was trying to tell you is I'm the only other person that could oppose him and stand a chance at deposing him. I know it, he knows it, and most of the court knows it. If I agree to marry you to him, it would unite us and give him peace of mind that I will not attempt to overthrow him. If I do not, I must be ready to fight and plunge the kingdom back into civil war."

Chapter Four

"Civil war?" I was back to a breath away from a full-blown panic attack. "Over me?"

I guess that wasn't fair, it was over politics, damn them all, but it felt personal. "So, somehow, I've thrown myself, and my friends from the frying pan into the fire? Figures." I stood up, displacing Mr. Mittens, and paced around the dining room.

My grandfather sighed. "This could just be a ploy at some long game the king is playing. He may only be inviting us to be polite and welcome you. We won't know until he tells us. But I thought that you should be prepared and a little more knowledgeable."

I threw up my hands, but that made me lightheaded, so I placed them on my waist, then bent over and took deep breaths. Once my head stopped swimming, I said, "Yeah, the politics seem simple enough, but how am I going to keep from offending anyone at court? I'm completely ignorant of the rules and traditions." I was amping up again and stopped to take some more deep breaths. "I don't even know what Mr. Mittens did that offended someone enough that he was banished." I waved at my cat, who hung his head. "If this is just a polite thing, the king could be watching me for the chance to use me against you. Did you think of that?" I said, my tone a little snappish. It wasn't his fault I'd landed in his lap and created a whole bunch of new problems.

"Yes, I've thought of that." He turned back to Dana who was still sitting with eyes downcast in her chair. "Did you bring it?"

"Yes, master." She stood and walked over to me. She presented me with a metallic bronze colored ball.

"What is it?" I asked her.

"A spell. Concentrated magic. You must swallow it."

"Why would I do that?"

Her eyes flicked to my grandfather.

He sighed dramatically. It had obviously been a while since he'd been around children, and I was feeling childish. I rolled my eyes.

"It is a spell to give you the knowledge of customs and traditions, so you won't cause any incidents."

I eyed the ball. It looked for all the world like a metal marble made of bronze.

"How long does it last?" I asked, assuming it was like a pill. You got four to six hours out of it.

"It is knowledge. It doesn't fade. You will understand, and for at least two days you will be unable to offend. A bonus from the magic. Everyone will find you—delightful."

I sensed a tiny bit of sarcasm. "Do I want the king to find me delightful?" I asked, seriously.

"Yes. The alternative would be catastrophic."

"But I don't want to marry him!" I whined. Now I sounded as childish as I felt.

"That is out of our hands. But whatever he plans, if you don't offend him, we are much better off."

I nodded. I plucked the offered ball from Dana's spidery fingers. I studied it. It didn't feel metallic despite its appearance. It was pliable and warm to the touch. Megan watched me with a frown.

"Should you eat that thing? You don't know what it will do to you. You know, you aren't really Fae," she said.

That was solid logic. I lowered my hand with the ball. "She's right. How do I know it's safe?"

Dana's eyes flicked to Mr. Mittens, he nodded and jumped up on the table to observe us all. His floofy fur was even fluffier and more alive in Faerie than on earth. His glow here was visible even in the light.

You have ingested a magic ball before. It did you no harm, he said.

"No, I haven't. I'd remember something like that."

It was the first time you came back to the house since you were a child. We had a painful encounter with your husband's mistress. She nearly killed you. Dana saved you and in return, you chose to have your memory erased. You swallowed a golden memory ball and forgot about magic for a time.

"No, that can't be!" Could it? I knew I'd purchased the house, looked at it and engaged the services of the Whelan's on a trip last year while my divorce was ongoing. But that time was fuzzy and murky in my memory. Was it because my memory had been messed with?

I trusted Mr. Mittens. If he said it was true, it must be. I could see myself doing it, too. I was overwhelmed at the time. My divorce settlement was being debated. Evan was yanking my chain, going back and forth from begging me to come back, then telling me horrible, hateful things. He and his she-devil mistress, now new wife, had just had a baby. I bought the house with no guarantee I'd be able to pay for it, and I was alone for literally the first time in my life. Magic would have just thrown me for a loop. It rang true.

What about Vanessa? I suddenly realized he'd said something about my husband's mistress being magical.

"My ex-husband's mistress is magical?" I blurted out.

She is a siren. A bird-like shapeshifter that lures men into marriages and slowly sucks them dry of desire, money, and life... Mr. Mittens said.

Seemed fitting. I wanted to smirk and be secretly gleeful, but I couldn't. Now I had to wrestle with my conscience over if I should tell him. Dammit. Well, I couldn't do a thing at the moment.

"Oh, she came to the house before I owned it fully?" I asked.

That is correct. She attempted to kill you. We prevailed. She was forced to take one of Dana's magic balls to forget her obsession with you. That is why she no longer troubles you, he replied.

Great, I owed Dana a favor. Vanessa had been the bane of my existence for a long time until I'd moved to my family's old house. I'd assumed it was only because of distance, not because she'd been bespelled. I'd take it though. If I never saw her homely face again, it would be too soon. Maybe she'd trip and fall off a cliff and I wouldn't have to tell Evan about her sucking him dry slowly. That made me smile.

Oh well. Thinking about this was a delay. I didn't want to eat the bronze ball. I didn't want magic giving me knowledge I wasn't sure I trusted. I trusted Mr. Mittens. I mostly trusted my grandfather, but only because I was sure he cared for me in his own way if only because he was obligated. But Dana? She was a wild card. She'd never been friendly; she was rude and harsh. I couldn't believe anyone with her fierce nature would bow and scrape to a master, so I didn't believe the show she put on for my grandfather.

On the other hand, I had little choice. If I didn't do it, I could get myself, my friends, and my grandfather hurt or killed, or *bonus!* start a civil war in Faerie. I was seriously screwed. I looked at Megan. Her eyes were wild and open, but she couldn't help me or make the decision. I popped it into my mouth before I could overthink it anymore and swallowed.

Megan gasped, then put her hands over her mouth.

I closed my eyes and wondered how long magic took to hit you. Was it like ibuprofen, thirty to forty-five minutes? Was it like…

Nope. It was pretty instant. One moment I was ignorant, and the next, a hot flash and I was full of knowledge on how to navigate the courts. In fact, I was being told to bow to my grandfather. How deep, how long, and how often. The compulsion was strong. I started to bend my neck but stopped myself.

"Will it be like this? A compulsion?" I asked through gritted teeth.

"For about two days, then it should wear off," Dana replied.

I felt the need to acknowledge her and heard myself say, "Your gift was well made and thoughtful." When my human mind wanted to thank her, the new knowledge forbade it. I remember my grandmother telling me as a small child that you never thank the Fae.

I fought off the desire to bow and asked my grandfather, "Do you have one for Mr. Mittens and Megan as well?"

He frowned at Megan. He hadn't wanted to acknowledge her at all. I remembered the sneer the king had given to Megan when he knew she was human, the scathing look at me until he realized I'd smelled Fae, and the disdain Dana had towards humans.

I sighed.

"Xrsrphn knows the customs and how to avoid trouble and notice. He is on very thin ice here. I had not thought to include your *human* friend in a trip to court."

"She goes where I go," I said, and Megan's jaw clenched. She was going.

He looked into my face, and his shoulders drooped slightly. "Dana, please prepare another knowledge ball for the human."

Dana turned and walked out after one of her "Yes, master" responses and a nasty look at Megan.

"Are you sure?" Megan hissed. "She's probably going to poison me."

"No. But I don't want us to be the cause of a civil war on another planet," I whispered back. "And she isn't going to go against my grandfather's wishes."

She shrugged but looked miserable. "Fair enough. Did it do anything to you? Make you sick or anything?" she asked.

"No, just a slight hot flash and the knowledge popped in my head, along with a sort of compulsion to obey that knowledge. I feel fine, if a bit weird."

She looked down. "Are you sure you want me to go with you? It sounds like I'm just a liability. The people here seem to hate humans." Her bottom lip trembled a little. She had to be scared and lonely.

I hadn't thought how Megan would feel. I was a terrible friend. I just assumed that she'd want to be with me because I wanted her around. In a terrifying situation, it was a solid and comforting feeling having your best friend. "I'm so sorry, Meg. I shouldn't have assumed. I want you with me, but do you want to go?"

She looked thoughtful. "I guess I want to go. At least, I don't want to be alone. If we piss off the wrong people, I want us to go out together. Blaze of glory, right?"

I laughed and looped my arm through hers. "That's right; we'll go out in a blaze of glory. Thelma and Louise style." The only problem was we didn't have a convertible to drive off the cliff.

Megan must have been thinking something similar because she said, "We might have to go over that cliff in a chariot or wagon or something else, but sure, why not?"

Chapter Five

Dana brought back the bronze ball within an hour. She plopped it into Megan's open hand, her lips twisted in disgust. At least she was consistently nasty. Megan's eyes slid to mine, asking silently for reassurance that it would work, not be poisoned, and she'd be OK. I didn't think I'd trust anything the Kelpie would give me if she wasn't working under my grandfather's orders. But she was, and for whatever reason, she seemed currently devoted to him, so I nodded.

Megan popped the ball in her mouth, and I watched her throat swallow reflexively. After a few moments, she gasped, "Oh my!" I grinned. The knowledge had hit her. She gave a little curtsy to me and Dana. "Oops, that is hard to resist," she said. "I guess that's good when we're at court."

"Yes, remember to listen to it, and obey. If you cause the master danger or embarrassment, I'll slit your throats and throw you to the dogs," Dana said encouragingly.

I shuddered.

Megan's eyes grew darker, and I knew her temper was flaring hot. I reached out a hand before she did something stupid. Luckily, the knowledge ball overrode her natural response, and she inclined her head, although her cheeks were flaming red, and her hands were clenched into fists.

My grandfather had left the room shortly after Dana, and he chose that moment to come back in.

"It is time." He gestured for us to follow, and we dutifully fell in behind him, eyes downcast as the compulsion commanded. Mr. Mittens trailed behind us. I had the feeling my cat was reluctant to go. We traipsed back to the room we'd used before to transfer between places. It was a cold, plain room with nothing but an inlaid, embossed, silver circle that filled the space between four walls. Once the door shut behind us and we'd taken our positions, my grandfather did whatever he needed to, and we were in a different if similar room.

"How does that work?" I asked in wonder. I'd been too tired and terrified the last time to ask.

He looked at me. "It is a simple transfer spell. It is worked into the circle and renewed often by technicians. You simply give it your pre-arranged word for the location you wish to travel to. The High Keep has thousands of pre-arranged locations loaded into it." He looked thoughtful. "If you ever need to travel to my fortress without me, the word is, Niamh."

I started. Niamh was his wife, my great-grandmother. He wasn't as unfeeling as Mr. Mittens made out. He had treasured her in his thoughts for many years if that's what he'd named his home. I smiled. Even Mr. Mittens seemed surprised, although it was harder to tell in his Ragdoll form.

"Can you go between the…uh…splinters?" That's what

Mr. Mittens referred to as the realms—splinters of reality—when he talked about realm walking, anyway.

Grandfather frowned. "Yes, but those aren't pre-loaded, you would need a very clear picture of where you wanted to arrive, and a strong magic *push*, for a better word, to make it happen. It is easier to use the pre-arranged locations."

I nodded. The information seemed important and could probably get us all home when my magic came back. I filed the fact away in my brain for later thought.

As we left the room and started down the marble corridor to wherever we were headed, Mr. Mittens pressed against my leg until I was afraid I'd trip over him. I didn't want to say anything because he'd seemed so out of sorts, so I walked a little slower than normal and more carefully. By the time my grandfather approached a closed door, we were several steps behind him and Megan.

They waited for us to catch up, then my grandfather opened the door. Unlike the grand court scene we'd been thrust in the other day, this was more like a private reception hall. There was still the throne on its dais at the far end of the hall, but there were far fewer people and courtiers hanging around. The king was seated on his throne, and he had two of his centaur guards behind and to the sides of the throne. A richly attired man in robes that looked like fire in stripes of red, orange, and yellow was organizing people. Another man that appeared to be an important courtier—dressed in dark, somber colors—stood next to the king, and a line of people waited to address the king. We joined the line.

When I peeked over at the king, he appeared bored, or he was talking and offering judgements on a variety of things, mostly disputes it sounded like. I tuned it out. I didn't even know enough to understand what people were arguing about. At one point, I caught the king's gaze upon us, and I shivered. He gestured to a servant, said something I couldn't hear, and pointed at us. The servant then hurried over to us.

"Come with me, please," he said as soon as he was close enough for us to hear. Then he scuttled over to a door next to the throne that I hadn't noticed before. It was the same color as the walls, and the only thing that distinguished it was a door handle.

He opened the door and gestured that we should enter. He closed it behind us. The room was small, like the size of an average bedroom on Earth, maybe ten by ten. It was painted a rich, mellow blue with comfortable seating and small tables spread around the space. A waiting room. I guess that meant we'd be here a while. I sank gratefully into a chair, lifted up my feet and rotated them around. Yesterday had been exhausting, and I still hadn't recovered. My legs were sore and felt like gelatin. My feet were bruised, and the little slippers weren't protecting them from the hard floors.

We quietly sat in the room, reluctant to speak. My stomach was an acid factory as we waited for whatever horrible fate awaited us at the hands of the High King of Faerie. Still, part of me was annoyed he'd called us here and made us wait for hours. But that was a common power play on earth as well. Mr. Mittens had initially sat at my feet, leaning against me, but as time went on, he jumped in my lap to get comforting pets and scratches. I think I caught my grandfather rolling his eyes at the antics of my cat. You could tell that my grandfather had spent time with earthlings. Eye rolling didn't seem to be a Fae thing.

When the door finally opened, I was almost relieved that my fate would be decided soon, because I was weary of waiting. I'd forgotten how it was to not be constantly entertained by an electronic device, but my phone was worthless here. I couldn't charge it, there was no internet, and I'd left it back at my grandfather's castle, anyway. I was almost disappointed when it was only a servant with refreshments, but by then we were pretty hungry, and even the state of my anxious stomach was grateful for something to eat besides itself.

We ate more colorful and unrecognizable Faerie food. When we'd finished, it was hurried away by yet another servant. The logistics of this place must be incredible. Finally, after what seemed like several hours and might have been, the head servant from the other room opened the door and beckoned us out. By then, I was sure I was seriously wilted, my clothing wrinkled, and my breath foul. Maybe that was good, and the king would take one look at me and decide that marriage was out.

Megan looked fairly good, and of course, my grandfather looked the same. We followed the servant back into the room we'd started in, only now it was empty of all but us, the fancy courtier, the servant, and the High King. He either was giving us a great honor, or he was making sure there weren't any witnesses. I wasn't sure. I shivered involuntarily.

This time, the king seemed more informal, less imperious. He addressed my grandfather, this time calling him Lugh rather than Pendragon. I watched carefully, listening to what the magic was telling me to do so I wouldn't offend anyone.

It compelled Megan and I to curtsy and look down. I did lower my eyes initially, but eventually I glanced up and looked around because I was dying of curiosity, and keeping my eyes on my toes was never my forte—unless a great pedicure was involved. Megan was also scanning the room, head still bowed. We caught each other's eyes and grinned.

We appeared to be inconsequential, though, merely chattel. The king and my grandfather were only focused on each other. This was an old struggle between two powerful Fae lords. Now that I knew the stakes, I concentrated intently on their conversation.

"I'm grateful that you came, Lugh," the king said. It sounded sincere to me, but then again, I didn't know him.

My grandfather dipped his head in acknowledgement.

"May we speak plainly?"

"Yes, my liege," my grandfather replied.

"I did not know you had another Fae child."

Even I felt that lie. He did know. This was the opening gamut of all the politicking and maneuvering I knew I was going to hate. Plus, I'd probably only understand a fraction of the underlying game, and that also pissed me off.

"As you know, my wife and my only child were from Earth." He gestured at me. "As is my great-granddaughter."

His eyes flicked to me, and I looked down.

"That is interesting. Does she take after her Fae heritage or her earthly one?"

Even though I didn't get the game, it made me sick to listen to it as though they were discussing my heritage like I was a prize horse.

"Though she is untrained, she has strong Fae magic," my grandfather replied.

I was growing angrier and angrier. Why was he answering and giving away all of my secrets? I didn't want to be stuck here in the Fae realm as someone's property, regardless if that made me a queen or not. I had a house I was turning into a bed-and-breakfast, a boyfriend to save, and a witch coven to defeat. I didn't have time for this.

"Would you consider her a worthy consort to someone like me, old friend?"

My grandfather looked miserable, but he answered with a simple, "Yes, my liege."

I wanted to slap him. I could feel the color rise in my cheeks and rage burn in my bosom.

I waited for my grandfather to offer up that I was not planning to stay, but he was silent.

The king turned to me. "Come forward, child."

Child? I was forty-two. I looked around in case I missed someone else that had snuck in while I'd been concentrating. There wasn't anyone but us.

I stepped forward, the magic inside of me compelling me before I could think. I walked forward, stopped, and curtsied. "My lord."

He studied me for a moment.

"How are you called?" he asked.

"Brigid, my lord."

"Brigid. He said my name slowly, testing it on his tongue. Show me your magic."

I looked at him confused. What did he want me to do, throw a lightning bolt at him?

"My lord?" I asked.

"Show me your best spell."

"My lord, that would be a lightning bolt, I don't think I should do that in here," I replied, uncomfortably.

He stared at me for a moment and guffawed. "Fair enough, child. Show me something small and controlled instead."

I'd forgotten that my magic had been stripped away, I reached for it, to show him a fire flower, but nothing happened. "I'm sorry my lord. When I accidentally realm walked us to this plane, I stripped away my magic. It has yet to regenerate."

His face was steely, waiting. I kept talking.

"I've just begun to learn, my lord, but I have lightning, fire, water, shadow, mind, reality, earth, aether, spirit, time, and light. Ice was stolen from me, and I'm missing air—at least I haven't found or re-integrated it yet," I said all of that so fast, I had to gulp a breath.

The king looked at me for a moment, then at my grandfather. "That is an impressive list. I didn't know that your family line consisted of thirteen elements, Lugh."

My grandfather gave a head bow but said nothing. The king seemed a little annoyed. Had my grandfather deliberately held out on him? That wasn't going to help our cause. Dammit. Why hadn't he warned me?

"I've other possibilities for a wife. I have another candidate who also claims her magic was stripped by an unintentional realm walk. Maybe I'll wait and see who's magic appears first," the king said sullenly.

My throat closed off, and I gasped for air. He had to mean Sofia. How did she get in a position to proposition the king? What was happening? Why hadn't something eaten her? Megan jabbed me in the ribs, I looked at her. Her face showed she was thinking the exact same thing I was.

The king took one look at my grandfather's face, which when I glanced over was suffused with rage. This was a political jab, and they both knew it. I wish I understood all the undercurrents to this meeting. It was frustrating. Plus, now I had to worry about Sofia coming into a place of power if he chose her instead.

The king waved a hand. "No matter." He sniffed as though he smelled something bad. "The other choice is unsuitable. She is also from Earth, as your great-grand-daughter is, but she is human."

Well thank God for small favors. Maybe the Fae penchant for unsubtle bigotry was a good thing.

"We will talk further," the king finished, and I wondered if he was going to make the offer for my not interested hand. But he dismissed us. I nearly fainted with relief, and Megan's quick squeeze of my hand let me know she thought we were off the hook, too. There must be better Fae candidates out there that weren't from Earth.

Boy, were we wrong.

Chapter Six

The official proposal was sent the next day by a court official. I was *officially* screwed. I couldn't see a way out of it, neither could Megan, Mr. Mittens, or my grandfather. I was going to have to marry the king. I could never go home again. I felt gutted. I didn't even have the strength to cry over my loss. If it didn't mean I'd destroy the kingdom and plunge it into civil war, I would try to go home the moment my magic came back, but it hadn't yet.

Mr. Mittens said maybe two weeks. It'd been three days. Two weeks was a long time to wait on a foreign world with no chance of escaping your fate, a bunch of murderous witches running loose on your property, and a missing Gabe. This was crazy. I couldn't help anyone, least of all myself. Plus, I'd gotten Megan stuck. Mr. Mittens could go back, although without me, there was no point. He was my protector, and I was the last of the line.

Hopefully, I could arrange to send Megan home soon. I'm sure my grandfather or Dana could send her, if she'd go. She could run the B&B herself; I could transfer the property over in her name. It was only fitting. I plunged into a deeper depression.

One of the things I was required to do before the wedding was attend classes on how to be a queen. Who knew there were queen classes? I would never in a million years guess that such a thing was a well, a *thing*.

The first day of classes, I had to leave Megan, while one of the king's Scáthanna centaurs picked me up.

"I'm so sorry, Meg. I wish you could go with me," I said once I was summoned to my grandfather's transporter room, as I called the place in my head. At least Star Trek had never let me down.

"It's cool," she replied, although she looked scared and afraid.

"It's not, but they won't let you or Mr. Mittens come."

She shrugged. "We'll find something to do. We'll put our heads together and come up with a plan to get us all out of here."

"OK." I couldn't think of a single way to accomplish that, but maybe they could find out about Sofia and her plans. "Can you two find out about Sofia?" I asked.

"That's an even better idea," she replied.

Finally, I turned to leave and follow the servant to the transporter room. It wasn't ideal, but at least we could work on our problems from different angles.

The centaur waited impatiently for me. She had a front hoof cocked and was leaning against the transporter room wall. She straightened up tall and fierce when I neared, and I wasn't sure if I was being escorted under guard or under arrest. As she followed me into the transporter room, I tried to get her to talk to me.

"Hi, what's your name?" I asked friendly like, although I felt like sobbing.

Silence.

"I'm Brigid. I've never met a centaur before you guys dragged us to court."

One scathing look.

"So, are there a lot of centaurs in Faerie?"

Exasperated sigh.

I wanted to ask even more personal questions like if there were male centaurs, if their hair was like a true mane, but those seemed intrusive.

"How fast can you run?"

If I kept up the endless questions, she might decide to answer one.

The centaur activated the transport.

Something occurred to me suddenly. "I'm so sorry, I didn't even ask if you can understand me or if you can speak."

"I can speak, but I'm on duty."

Yes, a win.

"Oh, that's wonderful. What's your name?"

I didn't know if eye rolling was a thing for the Fae outside of my grandfather, who learned it on earth, but I had that definite feeling she would—if that was done here.

"I'm called Sorcha."

Yes. "Nice to meet you Sorcha. How long have you been one of the royal guards?"

Another sigh, but she'd finally given in.

"This will be my second year as one of the king's Shadows."

"Shadows? Is that what Scáthanna means? Interesting."

"Yes."

We walked down the corridor, her hooves clopping on the hard surface, and her tail twitching with irritation, I assumed.

I noticed, now that I wasn't being death marched, and because she wasn't wearing armor today, that the centaur woman didn't have breasts on her human torso. They must be more horsey than human, and her mammary glands would be located where a horse's were. I didn't look or ask though. Must be easier to shoot a bow without breasts in the way, I surmised.

"How many weapons are you proficient in?"

"All of them."

"All?" I doubted she'd ever fired a gun. I might have laughed a little because she gave me a sharp look.

"Do you have to do a lot of training to make the elite guard?" I asked.

"Yes, it is quite vigorous and extensive."

"Are only centaurs in it?"

"We are *not* centaurs."

"You aren't? That's a term for half human half horse on earth. I didn't mean to offend. What are you called?"

"We are *Baincapall*."

I tried to pronounce it, and she corrected me until I got it right.

"I appreciate that you took the time to correct me. I don't wish to offend." I felt the compulsion of Dana's magic ball push me.

She inclined her head in a short acknowledgement and pointed me to a door. "Your class is inside. I will wait and escort you back."

I almost thanked her, but my magic manner pill was still working. "I'm grateful for our conversation."

She opened the door, and I walked through.

Inside was a team of people. I shivered. I was so far out of my element I wished I could flee. Apparently, it wasn't just lessons on manners and court rules.

I had to learn what to wear, how to do my hair, how to look, and who each courtier was and how to speak to them. I wished Dana had a magical pill for those too, but apparently, the pills were limited or no one thought about making one for this, hmmm.

At the first station, for lack of a better word, I was stripped and measured. My protests were completely ignored, and once the measurements were finished, I was bathed—although I'd done that before I came to court. I was scrubbed, oiled, and perfumed. I wanted to scream. The Fae must have a big thing with smells. I remembered the king sniffing us. Did humans really smell bad to them? I hadn't noticed any strange smell difference between our two races, but I hadn't been that up close and personal to any of them yet.

Once I was "clean," I was redressed in the Fae version of silken robes of a rich and beautiful color that reminded me of Megan's alexandrite pendant. The color changed in the light, and all the shades of purple, blue, and green shimmered around me. It was magnificent.

Then my hair was done. Apparently, curls weren't something the Fae had interest in, because time was spent straightening and smoothing my hair into a silky mass. My hair color wasn't common here either. My grandfather had dark red hair, but most Fae seemed to either have blonde or dark hair, and none had my mix of brown and red. At least the Lord of the Rings movies got that right. The hairdressers seemed to like to touch it.

This was the straightest I'd ever seen it, and it was longer than I thought, brushing over my waist. Their hair styles were simple, long straight hair, with a few elaborate braids on the sides and top to form fanciful shapes. Although for today, mine was simply swept back in a knot of four braids on top. It shone like a burnished dark copper when they were finished and contrasted with the soft robes I wore.

Next, how to stand, walk, and sit? I couldn't even remember all the things they wanted me to learn, and I was positive that I wouldn't tomorrow. I sighed. I couldn't do this, and I didn't want to either. There had to be a way out of it I was missing.

One interesting side effect of having so many people working on me and ordering me around was the amount of court gossip I got to hear. Most of it was just noise, since I didn't know anyone but my grandfather and the king, but when the gossip switched to the king, my ears were like radio antennas.

"He's having an affair with one of his Shadows," a whispered voice said somewhere behind me. My ears perked up.

I didn't want to think how that even happened with a creature who was only a step away from a horse, but who was I to judge?

"Really? I thought that was just vitriol," someone added from the other side of me.

"No, she's been bragging to the others and lording it over them."

"So, why did he choose this one?" someone whispered, thinking I couldn't hear.

"She's a powerful magic user."

"What about that Earth creature from the other day? You know, the one with the Swamp Lord?"

Could they be talking about Sofia? Who was the "Swamp Lord?" That sounded shady as hell. Talk about someone needing a bath and perfume.

JILLEEN DOLBEARE

"No, he turned that one away. The Swamp Lord was furious."

"I heard that he's trying to keep his Pendragon from overthrowing him," another said.

I was having a hard time keeping track of all the speakers, and I was starting to think they just didn't care if I could hear, or they knew it didn't matter because I was helpless to change my position.

"There's a rumor that..." Her whisper grew quieter, and I had to strain to hear. "...the Pendragon has more magic than the king."

There was a hush after that revelation. I shouldn't have answered the king on that one. I sealed my fate and my grandfather's with that.

"Yeah, someone said she has thirteen!"

"Thirteen? Is that the most in the kingdom?"

I lost the thread as my heart began to pound, and my mind went a million miles an hour wondering what that meant for us. If it was true, no wonder the king was intimidated and looking for a way to control my grandfather and me. Part of me wanted to say I only had eleven, but it wasn't really true. I was born with thirteen, and I planned to get them back. Part of me wanted to say I had none because I currently didn't have any. But I held my tongue. Once I came out of my state of despair, the conversation had moved on.

"There was another attempt last night."

An attempt at what, I didn't know.

"Really? Who caught it?"

"I don't know, one of the Shadows I assume, probably the king's mistress."

There was another discussion about if the rumors of a horsey mistress were true. I tuned out for a minute.

"The assassin actually made it into the king's chambers this time?"

My ears perked back up.

"He's dead now. That's one good reason to keep a deadly mistress," another said glibly. There were several titters of amusement.

My mind caught up with my ears. My heart raced, the king was dead? I wanted to cheer for a moment before I realized they meant the assassin.

"Nah, that can't be true, we'd have heard about it widely."

"You are wrong. He can't let anyone know that an assassin came that close to him; it would weaken his position and cause more to come after him." This came from an authoritative voice, and it took all my will not to look back for the speaker.

Seemed like logical reasoning. These servants probably understood court intrigue a million times better than I did. They needed to know to survive.

Before I could hear more gossip, the door opened, and an official came to retrieve me.

"If she is presentable, the king is ready for his audience."

It didn't sound like a request, and the team doing my "instruction" didn't think so either.

They scrambled with last-minute adjustments and hustled me out the door in two minutes.

I didn't even have time to work up a good head of terror before I was being escorted down a new hallway towards the king. However, by the time I made it to him, my hands were sweating, I was shaking, and it was all I could do to not burst into tears. What would he expect of me? Was this a private audience? Was I expected to perform "wifely" duties before the wedding? I was one suggestion away from a complete meltdown, and a shorter amount of time away from just choosing a direction and running. I wished fervently I had my cat and my bestie with me.

Before I cut and run, I was escorted into a chamber. I nearly collapsed with relief to see that I was not alone with the king. The room was full of courtiers and other important and officious looking people. The king sat on his throne, elevated in the middle of the room as usual.

I entered with the official and my *Baincapall* guard, Sorcha. I sure hoped she wasn't the king's secret or not so secret mistress. That would be awkward. I was announced, and I stepped forward and gave a deep curtsy. My knees almost collapsed at the bottom of it, my legs were still sore from the march two days ago, and I was weak and shaky from fear.

The king gestured, and the court official waved me forward to the throne. They had me positioned a step down. I turned to face the crowd.

The court official stood in front of the dais where the king's throne was and made a sweeping motion with his arm.

"Lords and ladies of the court! I present to you, Brigid of the line of Lugh, Pendragon to the king. She who will be queen!"

The crowd cheered and clapped. I'd expected them to bow or something, but apparently that wasn't appropriate for me, a nobody. Maybe they were really excited or faking it. Probably faking it. Although a wedding was probably a great big celebration with lots of free food. My stomach grumbled at that thought.

I smiled and waved, as the magic urged me to do, although inside I was screaming.

Once the announcement and subsequent waving, bowing, and scraping were done, the court official waved Sorcha over, and she escorted me back out and to the transporter room. She ushered me inside after checking that the room was empty, and I stepped into the circle. She said, "Niamh."

I felt the twist that indicated the magic had activated, and when I opened the door, my grandfather's walls greeted me, along with Mr. Mittens. He looked concerned. I squatted down and scratched his ears.

I should be allowed to accompany you, my pet, he said, his grumpy Ragdoll face even grumpier than usual.

"I agree. I could have used your company. It was awful. All dressing and having my hair done, and people telling me how to act. I much prefer you." I stood, and he walked me back to my room.

It sounds absolutely dreadful, he said.

I grinned. I'm sure Megan would also commiserate with me, so I had him drop me off at her room.

She squealed when she saw my dress and hair, so that made me feel good for a minute.

"How was it?" she asked and bounced a little on her bed where she'd been sitting when I came in.

"Just awful." I sat down next to her. "Not only did they re-bathe me—talk about humiliating—they talked over me like I wasn't there. I was pulled and pushed and ordered around. When I was done, I had to go to court and be admired and paraded about like a prize horse. I did, however, get a lot of court gossip."

"Do tell!"

"Most of the gossip was about people I don't know and I can't really remember, but the really juicy stuff was about the king. You know, the guy I'm being forced to marry? Apparently, his side piece is one of his horsey guards."

"I'm not sure what to think about that," Megan said, wrinkling her nose. "The horse thing is a bit cringe worthy. Also, are you ready to take on another cheating spouse?"

"Absolutely not. But you already know I want out of this and back home as quickly as possible. I find everything about being forced into this distasteful."

She put her arm around me and gave me a side hug. I rested my head on her shoulder for a moment. "Thanks, Meg. The only thing that makes this bearable is you and Mr. Mittens. I should probably make it possible for you to take over the B&B, and all of my other possessions so you can go back and enjoy your life."

"What? No! I'll go later, maybe we can both go back and forth! The king is gonna want time with his sidepiece, and you are only part of this for your ability to keep your grandfather loyal. Surely, he can't begrudge you time on Earth?"

I thought about it. Why would he? I was a political alliance, not some great love of his, or even a wife that could bear him children. As long as I was around for whatever queenly appearances I had to make, why couldn't I have a normal life back on Earth? I could learn to realm walk safely. I'd have to ask a boon of my soon to be husband. A tiny bit of hope and relief blossomed in my gut. I smiled.

"Yeah, why not?" I replied.

She smiled, and deftly changed the subject before I worked myself into another pit of despair. "So, tell me about your centaur guard? She looked terrifying."

"She is. Her name is Sorcha, and they call themselves, *Baincapall*, not centaurs. She was *offended* I called her a centaur." Then when it looked like Megan was going to pour on questions, I finished. "I don't know why."

"Ok, anything else we need to know about them?" she asked. I thought the same thing. If we ever had to make a quick escape, you should know your enemy.

"Yeah, they are badass. Sorcha said she was proficient with all the weapons. *All* of them. Their training is extensive. I'm thinking they are like special forces or something."

"All the weapons? What does that mean?"

I shrugged. "No idea. But remembering what we witnessed from them, and what I've seen my grandfather use, I'm thinking any medieval weapon is suspect. They already had crossbows, spears, probably swords and axes, maces. I don't know, that's about the extent of my medieval weapons knowledge, outside of like catapults and trebuchets. What does it matter? I'm only proficient at clunking someone over the head with a board."

"Have you done that a lot?" she asked.

I thought about it. Why had I said that? When was the last time I'd clunked someone over the head? I shook my own head. "I don't know where that came from. I do think I could do it, although a cast iron frying pan might be more satisfying."

She laughed. "Definitely, and it's cold iron—don't forget that."

"Next time I accidentally transport us to Faerie, I'll remember to pack one."

She snorted. "When we get back, we'll stock up!"

"Oh, another big thing. Sofia has hooked up with a dude they call the 'Swamp Lord.'" She has already petitioned the king for marriage," I said flippantly, as though it were an afterthought, rather than the most important information I had.

"Petitioned to marry the king or the swamp thing?" she asked, and I chuckled.

"King."

"Well, that sounds better than ole swampy."

I laughed. "Yeah. Much better." I sighed. "The king turned her down flat. He hates humans." I waved my hand around. "They all do, it seems."

"Yeah," she said.

We both flopped back on the bed. "I don't know about you, but I'm already tired of being here," I said.

"Yup. The food is good, but I'm giving it two stars for service," she said.

I shrugged. "I'm only giving it one star on Yelp.

Chapter Seven

I felt like I was in the movie *Groundhog Day*, since I had to wake up and go to "Queen" lessons every day, over and over. I was beginning to miss my magic lessons with Dana; they were less intrusive if you could believe it. Only, no magic, no magic lessons. Sad, since it would be much more convenient for her to instruct me here.

I hadn't been called into court again, so that was a relief, but I had to do whatever the equivalent of deportment was here. I had to learn to walk and talk correctly. The magic pill was still helping, but knowing why the pill told me what to do while I was doing it was helpful. I figured they only let me in court last time because they had to announce me, but it was too scary to set me free in court to screw up and embarrass the king and my grandfather.

Megan and Mr. Mittens had something up their sleeves, but they refused to talk about it to me, and I'd been too tired to push. The only thing they'd told me was they were looking into the "Sofia angle." Since I hadn't had time to do anything about that, I was glad someone was working on it.

The court gossip was along the same lines as the previous days. More dish on the king's mistress and more supposition about the assassin. Any mention of Sofia and Swampy had been abandoned. They really did dislike humans here. It sounded like the king had several assassination attempts a month. Why wasn't the Swamp Lord a suspect? He'd already tried to place someone in the king's bed. Seemed like a logical follow through to me. Would the assassination attempts affect me once we were married? Would I be on an assassin's list? The idea made my mouth dry, and my fight and flight response go into overdrive. I started checking the exits halfway through my sessions.

I did receive other pretty gowns. I figured the king or my grandfather were fronting the beautiful clothes. I had no idea how money or payments worked here.

The newest gown was just as colorful and unique as the last few. The difference was that instead of the cool colors, it was warm—a deep ruby red with shimmering orange and yellow iridescence, depending on the light. It made my hair look like dark fire. This time, they created an elaborate braided basket on top of my head, and no matter what they did to show me how, there was no way I'd ever be able to duplicate it. I assumed as a queen I wouldn't have to.

Sorcha continued to be my escort, which was cool since it had taken me so long to

encourage her to speak and took a lot less effort now that we'd been at it for a while.

"Do you like being one of the king's Shadows?" I asked first thing.

She sighed. Probably annoyed that I never stopped asking questions, but how was I going to learn anything if I didn't?

"Yes, it is the most elite unit in the realm."

"Who leads your group, after the king, of course?"

"Diamin is our leader. She is the best of us."

"Are you high up in the…" I didn't know the term. I didn't have any military experience outside of movies. "Group?" I added lamely.

"I am a leader of my…*group*," she said sarcastically.

"Sorry, I don't know the proper term."

"Together, we are called Scáthanna. We are grouped in tens. Those are called Deicheanna.

"Oh. How many of those do you have?" I didn't even try to pronounce the word which sounded surprisingly like Irish to me. I guessed the Irish and the Fae had ancient ties.

"Ten."

"So, there are a hundred of you all together?"

"Yes, are you curious, or do you intend to raise an army against us?" she asked. I bet she was worried. I had come out of nowhere, and the king was already worried about my grandfather, although surely the king's Pendragon already knew this info.

"Uh, no. You are completely safe from me. I couldn't fight my way out of a paper bag." I snort laughed.

Her brow wrinkled. "Paper bag? What is this thing?"

"It's just a dumb earth saying. It just means I'm a horrible fighter, sorry."

"Hmm. They are saying you're a powerful magic user."

"I don't know about that. I just found out I had magic, I've already had one piece stolen from me, I haven't found the last piece, and currently I have none because I realm walked without the proper preparation." I shrugged.

She looked at me sharply. "They are saying that your line contains thirteen elements. This is unheard of."

"Why, how many do most Fae have?"

She frowned. "I think the king has seven. That is a high

number. Most magic users have four or five. The weakest, one."

"Do all Fae have magic?"

"No."

"Do, *Baincapall* have magic?" I hoped I pronounced it correctly.

"We are made of magic."

"What do you mean, 'made'?"

She stopped and stared at me. "You are ignorant for the daughter of the Pendragon."

"I'm his great-granddaughter, and he only found out about me a short time ago."

"The *Baincapall* were created long ago by a powerful magic only a true Draoi can wield."

"Draoi?"

"Magic master."

"Like Dana? My grandfather's mistress of magic?"

"Yes, but she is not known for creating magical creatures such as the *Baincapall.*"

"What is she known for?" I asked, curious now.

"Portable spells."

"Like her magic balls," I said, but it wasn't a question.

Sorcha acknowledged that with a horsey sound in her throat. By then, we had returned to the transporter room. I grinned to myself. "Beam me up, Scotty," I whispered. The door was shut, so we had to wait for the transport that was currently happening.

Her sharp ears caught my comment. "Who is this Scotty?" she inquired.

"A great earth magician who could send people from ships to new planets with a tiny spell," I answered, no idea how to explain television or science.

Her brow wrinkled in confusion. "Between realms? He

is a great magician indeed. Few Fae are realm walkers, and fewer still can transport others."

I stopped. I'd taken me and three others on our trip to Faerie. Did everyone know that? Was I giving away something I should keep quiet? "How rare?"

She tilted her head in thought. "I've only ever known of three in all of Faerie."

I choked out, "Three?"

"Yes, why?"

I couldn't talk about it, so I mumbled something like, "just curious." I shut up. I'd definitely screwed my grandfather over by telling the king about my magic. He must have been keeping it all on the downlow for a long time. I doubted he was one of the three she knew of. I started to tremble. What had I done? I'd never get free now. I opened my mouth to ask another question.

Bam! I was thrown into the transporter room door, and Sorcha was knocked off her four hooves. Dust and rubble fell around us, and my ears rang. I was stunned. I looked around. Sorcha took a minute to get her legs under her. People were running and shouting. I heard Sorcha's name called faintly as though through water. I opened my mouth and moved my jaw to make my ears pop.

"Wait here," she commanded and galloped down the hall toward the rubble.

I didn't know what to do. I wanted more than ever to go home, but I didn't know what was safe, or correct in this situation. I didn't even know the situation, and my court knowledge magic didn't know either. I slid myself back up the door to my feet, leaned my back against it, and watched things unfold. More *Baincapall* galloped past me, with other normal foot soldiers running alongside.

I was still stunned, and there was so much noise and

confusion I couldn't figure out what was going on. My first thought was that Sofia had found me and brought an army to attack. That would explain the explosion, but that was stupid. It'd been less than two weeks, if my magic wasn't back neither was hers. Also, I doubted she could find more allies this quickly unless Swampy was continuing to help her —if she was even still alive after the king's rejection. I took a deep breath and tried to let that idea go. It wasn't her. This had nothing to do with me.

I don't know how long I waited, frozen and fearful. The next thing I saw surprised the hell out of me. The commotion moved until I could only hear muffled noise in the distance. I continued to watch down the hall towards the billowing smoke and rubble, when I caught a large figure striding down the corridor.

I blinked, confused. It was my grandfather. I didn't know he'd been at court today. He hadn't mentioned it earlier, and I hadn't seen him here at all. Not that anyone told me their plans.

"Grandfather!" I said in surprise. He was covered in dust, and blood trickled down his forehead. He just grabbed my arm and shoved me into the transport room. I stumbled in, hurt and shocked. I'd assumed the room was still in use, but it was empty.

"What's going on? What happened?"

"We'll talk when we get back home." He maneuvered us into the circle, took a deep breath, and said, "Niamh."

The room shifted, and we were in his home. He pulled me out of the transport room and shut the door. Then, he wilted like a huge weight had been lifted, and he could relax. He kept his hand firmly on my elbow, leading me to the room I thought of as his den.

I'm sure he could feel the questions burning through me with the force of my stare.

"Grandfather." Nothing. "Grandfather!" I repeated louder. Nothing. "Lugh!"

He shook his head and looked at me. He collapsed into his favorite chair, and I sat opposite, waiting. He leaned forward, elbows on knees, and scrubbed his hands over his face.

"You're bleeding," I said.

He lifted a hand to his forehead and looked at the blood on his fingers. He shrugged.

"I'm fine. There was an assassination attempt on the king tonight."

"What? Another one?"

He looked up at me sharply. "How do you know there have been others?"

"Court gossip. All the servants in my queen classes do nothing but talk to each other while they try to mold me into a Fae princess."

"Hmpf."

That startled me like the first time I'd heard Grandfather make that sound. So, like Mr. Mittens.

"Is that why you were there?" Part of me wondered if he had been the one to make the attempt. Was my grandfather interested in taking over the kingdom? He hadn't seemed to be. But he was there at the same time. What did it mean?

He considered me. "Do you think I would attempt to kill my king—without success?"

That question didn't help my doubt. "No?"

"I had a suspicion. I went to investigate it and discovered I was correct. I had nothing to do with the attempt. However, I think I might know how to stop a future one."

"Oh. Was it Sofia and the S-Swamp Lord?" I asked, terrified that my worst fear would come true.

"Who is Sofia?" he asked, alarmed.

"The witch who stole my power. Remember, I told you she was also accidentally brought here when I realm walked. She also petitioned the king for marriage."

I'd told him this the day after I learned about it when we were all at breakfast. He had brushed it away then, and he did it again. Being human really was dismissed here. Foolish. If any of them knew of human ingenuity and human weapons, they'd change their minds quickly. Their dependence and reverence for magic really made them blind to other things.

He waved the conversation away with a hand. "She has no magic then, and the Swamp Lord is only a minor threat. His magic is limited."

I thought that maybe he should look into them. Even without tons of magic, they could still gather an army or pay an assassin. I opened my mouth to say that, but he glared at me.

"Go, I must think." He waved me away after that. A clear dismissal. It angered me, but I wasn't going to get anywhere with him in this mood, so I stood and walked out and down the hall to Megan's room.

Chapter Eight

I let myself in and plopped on her bed. She was in the bathroom. I waited a few minutes, but when she didn't come out, I pulled the cord and ordered food when the servant came to answer the summons. Megan must be in the bath. I finally knocked on the door.

"Megan, it's me."

"I'll be out in a minute," she replied.

"OK, I ordered food."

"Thank heavens, I'm starved."

I could hear the tub drain. A while later, she opened the door, wearing a silky robe, her hair in a towel.

"How was queen class today?" she asked.

"Umm, it was fine, but afterwards was more exciting."

She eased herself into a chair with a groan and scrubbed at her hair with the towel.

"What happened? What's wrong with you?" I asked, concerned.

"Nothing. Just stiff from...uh, sleeping wrong," she responded.

I frowned, that was more than sleeping wrong. But I forgot it quickly in light of my news. "There was another assassination attempt on the king."

She stood up suddenly. "Oh no, were you there? Were you in danger?"

"No, I was waiting for the transporter room when it happened. It was chaos." I took a breath. "Then my grandfather showed up."

"No way, why was he there? Was he the one trying to kill the king?" she asked.

"No, but I thought that, too. Have you seen my cat?"

"Yeah, earlier." Her eyes shifted, and I knew she was lying about something, but I couldn't fathom why. "He came by to check on me. I think he hates not being with you when you're gone."

"He takes protecting me extra seriously."

"You don't get to change the subject. How do you know it wasn't your grandfather?" she asked, redirecting me back to the important information.

"He told me. He said he thinks he knows who's behind it though, and then he kicked me out of his den."

"Very odd."

"Either my grandfather is plotting against the king, or he is a loyal servant. I'm just not sure, but he doesn't seem like he's the kind that wants to rule the world. He seems more like me, mostly wants to be left alone to do his own thing."

She shrugged. "I guess. We can go get Mr. Mittens and have him weigh in."

"Is he in his room?"

"I don't know, but do you think he'd be hanging out with Dana?" She laughed, and we both shook our heads. "He's a cat. He's probably napping."

"True."

Before we went to check on him, I asked her, "Did you have a good day?"

She gave me the so-so sign. "I'm a bit sore."

"From sleeping funny?" I asked deadpan.

She looked away. "Yeah, something like that. Let's go check on your cat."

We both walked to his room, and I knocked.

There was a grumpy, *Come in*, in my mind. I cracked open the door.

"Mr. Mittens?"

Yes.

"Do you want to come eat in Megan's room with us?"

He looked up from his spot on the bed. He was in his natural form—four hundred pounds of exotic looking killer. Spotted like a leopard, sloped from his shoulders to hips like a hyena, with curved teeth that hooked below his jaw like a saber-toothed tiger, and a bobbed tail like a bobcat, Mr. Mittens was terrifying. However, when he saw me his eyes lit up. Maybe he was missing me, still feeling guilty, or missing his purpose. He hopped down and shifted into his Ragdoll form in the same motion.

I held the door for him, and he followed us to Megan's room.

Once the door was shut, I told him all that had happened on my way back. Then we started with our inter-rogation. "Do you think that my grandfather would plot against the king or try to kill him?" I asked point blank.

He did give me a few minutes of a thoughtful pause before he answered. *I have known your grandfather for a long time. I do not believe he has any ambition to rule a kingdom. I would be greatly surprised if he would do so. He's very loyal to his king.*

I breathed out a sigh of relief. That was what I thought

as well. My grandfather wasn't lying to me. He really wanted to catch the culprit. "Thanks, Mr. Mittens."

Hmpf, was his reply.

And since I'd just recently thought of it, and had no other current distractions, I asked him, "Who started that first, you or my grandfather?"

Started what, pet?

"The hmpf sound when you are annoyed or thinking?"

He cocked his head. *I believe your grandfather picked it up from me.*

That's what I thought. That small mystery solved, I brought up something else that was on my mind.

"Mr. Mittens. If I am stuck here forever, would you go home?"

He looked at me, his blue eyes wide and luminous. *Home, to Earth? No, while you are here there is nothing for me there.*

"No, home to your planet. The Splinter realm."

Splinter Realm? He chuckled into my mind. *There is no such place.*

"Well, what do you call your home?" I asked. Before he could answer, the servant arrived with our food. We set it up on a table and sat down to eat. My cat joined us at a plate and shifted into his Fae form to make it easier to eat with us at the table.

Mr. Mittens took a few dainty bites of finger food, and in between told us about his home planet.

"My home is called Xstlebdmnrdhgpl. I realize that is difficult for the human and the Fae tongue to pronounce. It means 'the true place.'" He ate another careful bite, as though it took concentration for him to eat in a humanoid form. "There is a legend among my people. There used to be only one realm. All that exists in the many realms existed once as only one people and one place. There was a great cataclysm. What caused it is argued about by our scholars. It might have been natural, or accidental, or a master plan, but the one realm splintered into millions of pieces. Each piece was a new realm and the people that had existed as one became another and spread among the realms to create new cultures, new creatures, and new people."

He grabbed another nibble. Megan and I were hanging on every word.

"We call ourselves the Xstlerphnm, it means those that walk the splinters. Many of our race and others from the other realms are able to realm walk. We can roam the splinters of reality."

Megan raised her hand. I reached out to pull it down, but Mr. Mittens raised one tawny eyebrow. "Yes?"

"Umm, you said not all of you could walk the splinters. Is it common though?"

"It is well known, so I'd say yes. It is a common skill among my people."

He grabbed a few more bites and continued.

"Brigid has this gift as does her grandfather. That is how he and I met. I was a young Splintercat, looking for adventures in the splinters as those of my kind often do. I wandered a few realms and found this one. It was very different and exciting compared to what I'd known. Its people balanced on two legs and were bare skinned rather than furred. I was fascinated. Since the people here relied on various items to barter with, I took a job as a type of bounty hunter so that I could provide for myself here. I'd hunt down dangerous creatures and bring them back for justice, or I'd kill them and bring back their heads for payment."

"How do the Fae pay you?" I blurted out. I'd been

thinking about it earlier but had no idea how currency worked here.

He gave me an annoyed glance. "They pay in bars of silver."

"Oh. Thanks." I looked down. I hadn't expected that. I thought it would be something more exotic, that was almost Earth-like.

"May I continue?"

I nodded.

"Your grandfather hired me a few times for the court. I became a top hunter for them. The last hunt I went on was for a unicorn."

"Unicorn? Like the one that tried to kill us?" I asked.

"Much like. Only this unicorn was hunting young, innocent Fae girls. Young innocent girls are the unicorns' favored prey. They have a common tactic. They graze in a field, acting like a regular pony. Most of them are silvery white when they aren't aflame, and their horns are crystalline and beautiful. So, they'll lure in a girl, act timid and shy, and make their way carefully to the unsuspecting maiden. Then when their prey is close, they strike."

I shivered and wiped my sweaty palms down my gown. "I'm not sure I want to know, but what do they do with the girls?"

"Unicorns don't eat grass," he answered, and the goose bumps raised on my arms.

I remembered the one we fought. They looked like handsome, stout ponies, but their manes, tails and legs were black flames. Their feet were clawed like a cat's, and their teeth were fanged. They were nightmares when they were trying to kill you.

"So, what happened when you hunted it?"

"There was a girl it was trying to lure in."

We leaned forward.

"I didn't know that at first; I was focused on the beast." He took a few more bites and launched into the story. "The unicorn made a horsey snort, and I froze, one paw suspended in the air. It was just blowing a piece of grass from its nose. Then it went back to fake grazing. I moved forward. Just before I could leap on it, a young girl—caught somewhere between childhood and adulthood—came into view. She squealed with joy, and the unicorn's head shot up. Its eyes lit with avarice. Times up, I thought and took the last few steps I needed."

He paused, and I wanted to smack him. Who knew my cat had a flair for story telling?

"I leapt; my powerful hind legs and my own magic carrying me forward." He lifted his hands, twisting them into claws as he spoke.

"To someone watching, it would appear I flew a short distance. I landed neatly on the unicorn's back. Unfortunately, unicorns are real bastards, as you've discovered. Not only did the unicorn's black flames light up, but it began to buck and throw its head around to dislodge me. Remember, it was my first time hunting one."

We both nodded, enthralled.

"I dug firmly into the unicorn's hide with my claws and tried to grasp its neck with my fearsome teeth, but before I could take the killing bite, the unicorn launched me into the air with a powerful jolt of its body. I twisted around to land on my feet. The unicorn barreled towards me, its head lowered, its wicked horn poised to skewer me."

I grasped my throat, my heart pounding with dread— which was stupid, he'd survived.

"I leapt away, and as the unicorn slid to a stop further down the field, I turned and raced towards it. By this time, the girl saw what was happening and started screaming for *me* to stop. Me! I scoffed, the silly thing didn't know that young girls were the unicorn's favorite prey. She just saw a pretty pony with a crystalline horn and went nuts. I was *saving* her from certain death! The unicorn turned, and we lunged at each other."

Megan grasped my hand, her eyes intent on my cat in his Fae form.

"To add insult to injury, the unicorn's flames had set the field on fire. The girl was in danger from that, too. If she was smart, she'd have run away. I wasn't flameproof either, although I was resistant in the realm because magic abounded, but my fur was getting singed.

"The girl finally ran away, right before me and the unicorn clashed. The horn slashed a burning path down my side. I yowled in pain, but the unicorn got the worst of it." Mr. Mittens lips curled up at the satisfying memory.

"My claws gouged a furrow down the unicorn's side, and it screamed its fury. I heal quickly, but the unicorn didn't have that ability. It also let rage rather than thought guide it. All I needed to do was wait for the beast to make a mistake."

He paused and took a long drink from a bowl of cream. Megan tapped her fingers on the table. "What happened?" she finally asked after he'd stalled longer than her patience would allow.

My cat continued, "For all its reign of terror, the unicorn was young. Its rage caused it to make its very last error. It whirled and charged me again, and that's when I broke its neck with a careful swat of my paw. I left the body lying in the field. Before the fire in the field consumed it, I snapped off the horn with my teeth as proof of death and *walked* back to my employer, your grandfather." He inclined his head at me.

"Something happened here. It must have or you wouldn't have ended up in the human realm," I chided him.

He looked at me with a tilt of his head, but he continued.

"Since I couldn't realm *walk* within the same realm, I stepped to my home realm, Xstlebdmnrdhgpl, and back to the Fae realm outside the door of the home of my employer, a certain Fae lord. I didn't know the lord's name then because that wasn't done here—I didn't know why at the time. I thought that maybe their names were hard to pronounce since I'd noticed that people from other realms struggled with my name." He shook his head at his own ignorance.

"Since it was polite, I shifted into my new Fae form." He gestured to his current shape. "Splintercats like me aren't fond of two-legged forms. They are ungainly, and you two-leggeds tip over easily even if you are a perfect specimen of feline grace like me."

Megan and I tittered. He was definitely a cat. He was so full of himself.

He glared at us for a moment, then continued, "I took a moment to make sure I was centered and called the servant to announce me. I was new to the culture, but I'd figured out that was what you did here. I had a firm grasp on the horn in my hand. The servant escorted me to your grandfather's sitting room."

He pointed down towards the room I'd dubbed my grandfather's den.

"Your grandfather had me join him by the roaring fire."

I looked at Megan. She grinned. Cats liked nothing more than a warm spot.

"Before I sat, I handed the horn to my employer. He examined it, the light from the fire dancing over its crystalline beauty and sending prisms of light shooting over the room. I itched to bat at the light, but I gripped my hands together." He took another drink.

"Your grandfather recognized it was a young unicorn but believed it was the one he'd sent me after. He sent a servant to retrieve my payment and deposit it in my accounts. While we waited, he asked me for a favor. The thing that was to become my downfall."

We waited for him to continue, but before he could there was a knock on the door.

Damn cat and his dramatic pauses, I huffed to myself as I reached out to open the door. I expected a servant since that was all that had ever knocked on our door or come to see us at all.

I jerked it open with an imperious "Yes?" on my lips.

It wasn't a servant. It was my grandfather in the flesh and flanking him was a bored looking Dana. I invited them in, a questioning eyebrow raised.

Once the door was shut, Dana did something magical. I felt it ping against my ears like a pressure drop.

"We needed to meet in secret." My grandfather looked around. "Whatever I say here cannot be revealed to anyone, do you understand?"

We looked at each other and agreed.

"You are aware there have been several assassination attempts against the king?"

We mumbled, "yes," waiting.

"I've uncovered those involved in the plot, and I'm going to need your help to bring them down."

For some reason, that caused my throat to go dry and my hands to sweat. "How?"

"First, we are going to need your magic."

I looked at him, my brows scrunched and my eyes narrowed. "How? It was stripped away."

"I've had Dana working on a renewal spell. It has never been done successfully, but we might have found a work around."

"So, I have to take one of Dana's untested spell balls?"

"Precisely."

"Even with my magic, I'm worthless. Just ask Dana!" I protested.

"She believes you are competent in the area we need."

My eyes drifted over to her. She didn't acknowledge me or agree with him. She just stood there, staring, her poker face utterly blank.

I sighed and paced around the room. "What is it you think I can do?"

"I need a lightning bolt."

Chapter Nine

"A lightning bolt? Are you nuts? I can't control those things! I could kill you, the king, or a lot of other people, slinging around lightning!" I protested. "Can't you do one?"

He stared at me stonily. "I can, but it can't come from me. We may only have one chance at this, and we might need it. Besides, we have yet to see if Dana's spell can renew your power or not."

He waved her over. She held out her hand, a shiny blue ball in it.

I sighed. "If it doesn't work, what will happen?" I looked directly into her eyes.

"The worst-case scenario...you will vomit." She looked thoughtful. "Perhaps pass out. Maybe die." She looked a little too happy at that prospect.

"Die? Do I have to sign a release?"

"What is that?" she asked.

"Nothing. An Earth thing," I answered, my sarcasm going over her head.

I looked at Megan. She was staring at the ball and

shaking her head. "You shouldn't do this, Brigid. Even a slim chance of death is too much!"

I looked at my grim-faced grandfather and Dana with her horsey smirk and grabbed the ball. I didn't want to think about it. But if it renewed my magic, maybe I could realm walk us home if I had to—you know, in an emergency. Being without my magic was too risky. I could die anytime I was at court. Who was to say an assassin wasn't going to be waiting for me next time?

I tossed it to the back of my throat, grabbed the fruity beverage I'd been drinking, and swallowed. I felt sick. I wasn't sure if it was from the magic ball or the anticipation of death. I burped up a little acid. So, maybe it was the ball. All I could do now was sit and wait. Megan and Mr. Mittens looked on with something akin to horror on their faces. Would Dana be happy or relieved if I died? Would my grandfather?

We were all silent for approximately ten minutes, waiting, when Dana broke the silence. "It was only a very slim chance of death. Whatever is going to happen has. Try something, Brigid."

I didn't feel anything different. No rush of power, no hot flashes or sprays of mist, nothing. I held out my palm, concentrated through my ring, and attempted to pull up a flame. I probably should have started with water, but flame seemed more appropriate.

It was like flicking a lighter. My flame sputtered to life a few times then died. I looked at Dana.

"Continue."

I took a deep breath and concentrated. Finally, a steady flame appeared. It was weak and took a lot of effort.

"Good," she said.

"That was weak. I can barely do it. I doubt I'll be able to summon a lightning bolt."

"Your magic is restarted, it will grow now. You should be restored by morning."

"So, it's like a battery?" Megan asked. "You just jump start her and if she keeps the car running, it will return to full strength?"

The two Fae looked at her, confusion on their faces. My grandfather had to have had some experience with cars, but he might never have known how they worked or what the battery did. The analogy worked for me though. I nodded.

I only knew very generally how a combustion engine worked, but I tried to explain. "A battery provides an electric spark—like a small jolt of lightning—which ignites a flammable liquid in a car engine, and that drives pistons up and down that then turn all the rods and things in that engine to make it go forward." The blank looks continued. "When the battery goes dead, another battery can charge it, so it'll spark again. If the engine runs for a while, it will recharge the battery fully." I didn't want to explain an alternator, so I left it at that.

They didn't get what I was talking about, so I dropped it. It didn't matter; my magic was back. And all I had to do was wait, and my magic would be recharged.

"I appreciate the effort it took to make that ball, Dana," I said to her. My courtly magic pill still suggesting the appropriate responses.

Her mouth might have twitched briefly into a smile, but I wasn't positive.

"Do you feel sick at all?" Megan asked.

I thought I was fine, and the twinge of nausea I had after I took it seemed to have passed. "I think I'm good."

She looked relieved, and we sat at the table to discuss plans to stop the assassin.

"Who is the assassin?" I asked. I figured we might as well get the ball rolling—no pun intended.

"I believe it is his Phoenix."

"Phoenix? A magical bird that dies and resurrects from fire?" I asked.

"What? No, the king's most trusted advisor," Grandfather said.

"So, Phoenix is a title," Megan mumbled. My cat continued to eat, not interested.

"Have we met the Phoenix?" I asked.

"You have seen him at court. He was the one announcing everyone and directing the supplicants."

"The guy in the fire robes?" I asked, remembering back.

"Yes, those are the robes of his office."

"Why would he want to kill the king?" I asked. "Is he next in line for the throne?"

"He is a contender, although killing the king would be only the first step in a series of challenging tasks to replace him," Dana added.

"So, how do we prove it's him and stop him?" Which really was the most important thing.

"Cautiously. If I'm found around him and something goes wrong, I will be blamed. If we fail to stop him, and I get caught, I will be blamed. If for any reason we cannot prove it is him and stop him I'll…"

"Yeah, you'll be blamed." I finished for him. A small wave of fear for my only relative flashed through me.

"Correct."

We looked at each other.

"What about Sofia and the Swamp Thing?" Megan asked.

My grandfather wrinkled his brow. "The Swamp Lord?"
She nodded, with a twinkle in her eye.

"They do not have the power or the fortune required to hire elite assassins," he said dismissively.

"Alright. I guess that could be true." Megan sighed. "If this were earth, we'd just put up some cameras or hide a microphone or something."

That was true, but it reminded me of something. The witch's bug. When we'd been spying on the witch coven, Megan had snuck in to break the ward on the building they were in. She was successful, but when she came back, we'd found that the ward had implanted a tiny insect looking tracking device on her. Compared to what Dana did with her magic balls, it was primitive at best. Unable to record or take images, it could only report where someone was, and probably didn't have a huge range.

"I think I might have an idea," I said. "Meg, do you remember the bug?"

"Bug?" she asked, thinking, then her eyes lit up, "Yes! At the witches' warehouse."

I turned to Dana. "The witches had a small magical device." I held up my fingers to indicate the size. "It looked like an earth insect." I shook my head; she might not know what an insect was. "Do you have insects on Faerie?" I asked. It was a stupid question, I remembered brushing some away when we'd been marching to the king's palace.

"We do," my grandfather answered. "Please continue. This sounds intriguing."

"So, we were trying to spy on the witches." I looked at my grandfather. "You know, the bad ones that stole my magic."

He inclined his head in acknowledgement.

"So, we couldn't get into the place they were in because it was warded against magic users."

Both he and Dana appeared confused with the word warded, and I remembered that Fae didn't have wards in their repertoire.

"Uh, a ward is like a magic bubble that keeps out whatever you have warded against. In this particular case, magic users."

"So, we sent Megan in because she isn't a magic user, and she broke the ward so we could enter. But when she did, she came back with a bug on her. It was made to keep track of where she was, but that was all. We found it and removed it. This is the part that is exciting. It was crude and limited, but since Dana's specialty is portable magic, perhaps she could design a bug that could record sound or images."

We all looked at Dana expectantly. She looked perplexed. "I do not understand images or record."

I looked at Megan, and she at me. "Does your phone still have a charge?" I asked.

She shrugged. "I don't know. I turned it off when we arrived here."

"Me too. We can see. That would be the best way to explain it to her. Where's yours?" I asked.

"In the bathroom, under my clean earth clothes," she said.

"I'm going to go get mine. Hopefully one still has enough of a charge for this to work."

I left and hurried down to my room, retrieved it, and returned to Megan's room. She already had hers. "Ready?" I asked. We both hit the power buttons and waited for the phones to turn on. The moment of truth. Mine had been fairly full when we'd gone up against the witches, and I'd turned it off before that. We'd been dumped in Faerie several days ago. I'd never turned mine off for longer than a few hours, and I didn't have a clue if they retained a charge when they were off. I held my breath.

The tone sounded, and both phones lit up. My grandfather had looked at mine before when I'd shown him a picture, and he had remained curious because he leaned in to see the device. Mine was slightly more than half full. I looked at Megan's. It was more than three quarters full. We bumped fists.

"Ok, I'm going to show you what record means, Dana." I flipped to my camera feature and hit video. "Dana, walk over to the closet and come towards me and say something while you do it, please." I tacked the courtesy on at the end because her frown was angry and terrifying.

She dutifully stood up and walked over to the wardrobe. As she started towards me, I hit record.

"This is a pointless and ridiculous exercise," she muttered as she walked. Once she was by the table, I ended the recording, and then turned the phone so both Dana and my grandfather could watch. I hit play.

I could hear the tinnier version of Dana's voice through the small speaker, but Dana and my grandfather's reactions were violent and priceless. They reeled back, my grandfather jumped to his feet, and the chair crashed behind him. Dana lifted her hands, probably to blast the device with magic, but I stopped her.

"This is a recording with sound and images. This device is made with human knowledge of machines like cars, Dana." I'd taken Dana for a ride in a vehicle, and it had scared her. It'd gone too fast, and she couldn't handle it. But, before we'd gone on our ride, I'd told her it was a machine made by people without magic. "It isn't magic. Do you think you could replicate what it does *with* magic?"

Dana took the phone from my hand and looked it all over. She tried to peer inside the charging hole, but that was useless. She handed it back. "I do not know. I didn't know such a thing was possible. I will have to think."

"What do you think, Grandfather?" I asked.

He shook his head. "It is a marvel. If anyone can figure it out, it would be my Dana."

Dana had remained frozen in a state of thought. Suddenly, she looked up and announced. "I must go to my lab."

My grandfather excused her, and she left.

"I guess she had an idea," I said.

Everyone agreed.

"If this works, we have a way to prove your Phoenix is dirty," I said. "We will record him and give the recording to the king. Then we will be free to help him bring the traitor to justice."

My grandfather looked as though a weight had been lifted. The entire plan was weak, but it was a start. If we could stop this, maybe the king's trust in my grandfather would be renewed. Who knew? Maybe he'd be willing to let me go home once in a while.

Chapter Ten

Dana came through. It took her three days of tinkering, and no one was allowed to disturb her. I continued with my queen classes; grateful no assassination attempt was made on me. I tried to listen harder to the gossip, desperate to see if anyone suspected the Phoenix or for more news about Sofia and the Swamp Lord. But the gossip was hard to focus on, there were too many people in the space working, too many voices to try to separate. I considered just asking, but I didn't want any suspicions getting out before we were prepared.

Sorcha continued to be assigned to me. I was becoming more and more comfortable with her, and I thought she was more comfortable with me. I wondered if it would be appropriate to ask if she could help us, but I figured I'd run that by my grandfather first. It was his neck most at risk unless he fled the kingdom with us. That wasn't a long-term solution for him though, he couldn't stay on earth for longer than a week or two without deleterious effects. The magic there was weak, and the atmosphere was thinner than on Faerie.

Dana called us into my grandfather's den. Her long horsey face and shark black eyes were alight with anticipation. She must have pulled it off to look so pleased and excited to show us. Her horsey ears twitched constantly with her poorly concealed anticipation to unveil her toy.

When we were gathered, she pulled out a thing about the size of an average earth beetle. About three-quarters of an inch long, it had a dark carapace that shimmered with iridescence like many of the things here in the Fae realm. The Fae seemed to have a love of multiple colors that changed in different types of light. It reminded me of corvid feathers. They appeared black until the light caught them, then they glowed in purples, blues, and greens. She moved the beetle thing back and forth so we could see the color change then launched it into the air. Its wings parted, and it flew like a beetle did as well.

"Is this a common insect here in Faerie?" I asked.

"Yes," my grandfather said, watching it with curiosity.

Dana watched us watch the beetle; her eyes lit up with delight. She let it fly around the room, then opened her hand. It came back to her and alighted, wings folding back under the hard shell.

"Is that all it does?" Megan asked. I swatted at her hand next to her side to get her to shut up before Dana annihilated us with a twitch of her power.

Her eyes went from excited to pissed off in an instant. "No, that is not all it does, insolent human."

"Sorry," Megan muttered. "I thought that was pretty impressive."

Dana then stood and approached my grandfather. She placed the beetle right between his eyes, he froze and gasped a little. Once she let go, the beetle's inner wings spread to form delicate spectacles that covered his eyes. His body twitched with shock, and then wonder. After several moments, the wings furled back into the beetle's body. She plucked it off the bridge of his nose and looked at me.

"OK," I said before she could ask. My curiosity overwhelming the ick factor.

She approached me, and my eyes crossed, watching her place the beetle on the bridge of my nose. I closed my eyes and fought off the urge to swat it off my face. Its magic hummed. I opened my eyes as the wings unfurled and was presented with the beetle's view of the room as it buzzed around watching. It replayed our conversation. It was miraculous that she could create something like this without microchips or the knowledge of video players. The replay stopped, and the wings furled. She plucked it from my face. She looked at Megan to see if she wished to experience it, but she shook her head and put up her hand. She'd been wary of insects since the Soul Spider incident. Dana even offered it to my cat, who also declined. He seemed bored.

"It's brilliant!" I exclaimed after Dana folded it back into her hand.

She almost cracked a smile.

My grandfather was strangely silent, but he must have been thinking.

"That beetle." He gestured at her closed fist. "How long can it fly and re-re-cord?" he stuttered over the strange word.

Dana frowned for a moment. "I'll have to perform further tests, but my crew is producing five more of these delightful *bugs*." She emphasized the word, since it was one we had introduced to her. "So, we will have better specifications soon. We will need to destroy one to see what their capabilities are to the fullest."

"Crash test dummies," Megan mumbled, and I suppressed a laugh.

"How soon before we can use them?" he continued.

Dana gave a slight frown. "Another day, maybe two."

We could tell he wasn't happy that it would be so long, but he gave her a weak smile. "Perfect, make it so." The dismissal was cruel and obvious to all of us. My shoulders stiffened as I saw the light in Dana's eyes go out. She went from cherished team member to servant in an instant. Rage lit up my heart. He'd just treated her like Evan used to treat me.

Her shoulders hunched, but she turned and left. I watched her shut the door behind her carefully.

I couldn't stand for that. I had my issues with Dana, but I had more with abuse. "Grandfather, I know this is not my place or my business, but you just destroyed her with that dismissal. She created something impossible in a very short amount of time. I know that this is time sensitive, but she is more than a servant, and you've made it clear she is less than your equal with that one statement. I don't know if you want to turn her against you. She is deeply loyal to you, and my experience has shown that praise and care go further than what you just did."

He frowned at me, and I was sure he would strike me or reprimand me. But he looked at the door and sighed. Then he turned and looked at me with a little fire in his eyes.

I took a step back.

He shook his head. "You are correct. It is not your business. However, I'm not unfair. I will make it right."

He gave us a curt nod and left to follow Dana.

We did not need her to join our enemies. We had to

keep her firmly on our side. Plus, I couldn't tolerate any type of emotional abuse. Although what he'd done was small, it still hurt, and I understood that better than anyone.

"Well," I said to Megan and Mr. Mittens. "I guess we should eat and go to bed. There's nothing else to do until Dana has the finished products ready."

———

Although every day that passed, the desire to return home and check on Gabe and my house only intensified, but we couldn't do anything except wait for Dana's "bugs" to be ready. We had to stop the plot against the king. At least she'd been right about my magic, and it seemed fully restored—at least the eleven pieces I had. Now, in between tedious queen lessons, I added in magic lessons with Dana. In the few short hours we had, she needed to teach me how to better control lightning—the scariest and least manageable of my powers. I guess grandfather wanted to keep his plan on the back burner in case the new plan failed.

Dana wanted me to learn the smaller applications like shocking someone and creating a throwable ball of electricity. The only time I'd used my lightning to shock someone was because it was being repressed by witches. If I tried it now, I'd turn someone to ashes. To say I was scared to experiment was an understatement.

I explained that to Dana. She laughed in my face.

"Look around, child," she said. "This room is shielded from all magic. You will be able to wield your power safely, and no harm will come to either of us."

"Then how will you know if I'm doing it right?" I asked, confused.

"You will see. Now, aim your power at that spot." She

pointed to what amounted to a target on the other side of the empty room. I didn't see how this room would suppress anything; it looked just like a basic room, nothing special. The only thing in it was the target on the wall, and us.

I gathered my will, focused it through my ring, held up my hand, and aimed at the target. I let a lightning bolt fly. It was odd, to say the least, the room did suppress my magic in a way, but not the way I was expecting. The bolt blasted from me as strong as always, but it wasn't lightning. The room changed it into light. So, it seared our eyes, but no killing force blasted into the wall, missing the target by ten feet. That was what I was afraid of. I couldn't aim the bolt like I wished; the lightning arced the way it wanted.

"That is pathetic," Dana, the best teacher in the world, encouraged. Even said directly into my head it sounded sarcastic.

"I know," I breathed out in a disappointed sigh.

"Again. This time try throwing it, not aiming it with your hand. Can you throw straight?"

In other words, "you throw like a girl."

"No."

She huffed at me.

"Try anyway."

One thing about Dana's method of teaching. She was harsh, but she didn't play games. She called it as she saw it.

She was just going to call me inadequate which I was, so I gathered a ball of electricity into my hand, as she'd shown me, and threw it at the target. It went from my hand, arcing down, and hit the ground well short of the target. I'd warned her.

An exasperated snort came from her horsey face. I rolled my eyes. "You are correct. I would have to teach you to throw properly before that is worthwhile, but we'll continue to practice building it up in your hand, you could just smash it into someone's face. Try the bolt again."

It was pretty sad when one form of defense was off the table because you grew up being bookish rather than tomboyish. I built the magic in my mind, aimed my hand, and fired. I did that until I could barely lift my arm anymore, and although my aim improved, I never once hit the target.

"We'll continue tomorrow," she said finally. Her sigh and the shake of her head let me know how completely disappointed in me she was.

I didn't have the motivation to even respond. I just stumbled out the door, wondering if I could even help my grandfather at all.

Chapter Eleven

The next day, I remembered to talk to my grandfather about Sorcha before queen classes and torture with Dana. I called the servant and had her contact him since I didn't know how to find him or where he was in the castle.

It was early by Fae terms, but he was already up and working in his den. Plans of the high king's keep were spread over the table near the bookshelves, and he was poring over them.

"Grandfather," I addressed him to get his attention.

His eyes drifted up to me. "Yes, child?"

I hemmed and hawed a bit, not sure how to bring this up. "I've sort of made friends with one of the king's Shadows, and I was wondering if you want to bring her in on this. Maybe she could help get close to the Phoenix, where you and I would struggle?"

He stared at me, but I could see the wheels turning.

"That could be a great risk," he said.

"I know. I think we can trust her. She is loyal to the king and would want to see him protected."

He nodded, unfocused as he continued to think.

"She knows I'm not a threat, although I don't know what she thinks about you."

"That is a problem." He looked down at his plans for a moment. "Do you think she would be willing to come speak with me? I might be able to convince her. Show her the bug and the plans?"

"Yes, but what if she won't agree after you speak?"

"Then, we'll have Dana give her a forget ball."

"She's a highly trained weapon, how would we do that?"

"We have ways; Dana can accomplish it."

I looked at his face, it was firm, but his eyes twinkled a bit. He had a lot of faith in Dana's abilities, and it showed in his subtle expressions. He even looked forward to Sorcha failing and having to turn her into Dana, huh?

Still, I knew Dana was his Mistress of Magic, but I didn't think she was some badass weapon like Sorcha, so a little trickle of fear ran through me. She was scary. Maybe Dana liked me more than I thought, because she was free to do anything to me when I was with her. But now? I was terrified to be alone with her. I'd always shuddered a little to be near water when we worked at my waterfall since she was a Kelpie, but now I could never work there with her again, if I ever got to go home. Even if I could hold my breath for forty-five minutes or more.

"OK, I'll ask her if she'll come, invite her for tea or something."

"It has to be today; we launch the plan tomorrow."

"Yes." I looked at him and glanced at the plans on the table, they just looked like drawings and useless words to me. "Thanks, Grandfather, I've got to go to queen class now."

He looked back down at his plans, dismissing me.

I hurried to the transporter room since I was a little later than usual. I loved saying that. I'd always loved Star Trek growing up.

Sorcha was waiting at the door to pick me up. My loyal guard. Only she was there for two reasons, to protect me and to keep me from doing anything I wasn't allowed. A double-edged sword.

She wasn't very talkative, and I was curious, so I asked her what was wrong.

"There has been another attempt on the king. We've been on high alert today, not much sleep in my past or future," she said.

"That's terrible! I'm so sorry, my friend." This looked to be the perfect opening to invite her, give her a bite, and let her be a hero. "What if I told you I could help with that?" I asked.

She stopped and whirled on me. "What do you know? Is your grandfather part of this?" she hissed.

"What? No! But we have an idea on how to catch the culprit. I was going to ask you today if you wanted in. If you could help us."

Her eyes narrowed.

"What would be involved?" she asked, still suspicious.

"Come for tea? We can talk with my grandfather, and he can show you what we plan to do."

"Tea?" What is that?

"It's a drink made from leaves, it's an Earth thing. You can drink whatever you want, or not drink, it's just a saying. I'm inviting you over for light refreshments and the chance to save the king."

"Why would you want to save him?" she asked. It was a great question. The truth was I'd be out of the marriage and on my way home if he died. She knew I didn't want to do this and that I wanted to go back to my realm.

I thought a moment more, planning the best way to answer. "Because if that happens, this realm will be thrust into a huge civil war. My grandfather would be fighting, and I could lose him. I just found the one family member I have left in all the realms, and I'll do anything to keep him as safe as possible. He is loyal to your King, even if I couldn't care less about the problems of the kingdom. That's why."

She looked at me, a frown deepening on her face. "I will come."

"I think you'll be pleasantly surprised at what we're going to do."

That arranged, my heart lifted, and I strolled happily to my gossiping session with the courtiers. After a little makeup, hair, and dressing by my gossipy pack of servants, I was ready to get the dirt on our target. Boy was this place a hotbed of intrigue. I was going to pay close attention, and not let them distract me from finding out about the assassin, the king's Phoenix.

Sorcha dropped me off at my session and wandered off to do whatever she did when she wasn't with me. I sighed and opened the door for my torture session to make myself court presentable.

The servants were all a titter today, their tongues wagging about the new assassination attempt. One thing was sure, it was hard to keep a secret from the servants. They saw everything because they were everywhere.

The one doing my hair was deep in the description of what happened to the king with the lady doing my face. "He leapt out from behind the wall hanging in the king's chambers. No one knows how he got there!" she exclaimed.

The hair lady paused, her fingers deep into my curls, attempting to smooth them.

"Oh my, what was the weapon this time?" face lady asked, swiping color on my cheeks.

"Magic, no physical weapon. He tried to burn the king to a cinder."

"What did the king do?"

Hair lady started tugging on my scalp, braiding my hair into some elaborate net. "Well, the king is apparently a fire elemental as well along with his other powers. So, he extinguished the flame and called his Shadows in. The chambermaid said she'll be cleaning blood off the ceiling and walls for days!"

I swallowed hard. They were vicious, the king's Shadows, and I wouldn't want them angry at me. At least that assassin was done for. How many could be hired before the pool ran low? I shook my head. The serving lady tugged hard. "Hold still, please, milady," she asked politely, although I could feel the desire to rip strands of hair out through her hold.

"Forgive me, that news was disturbing."

"Of course, milady."

You'd think my comment would quiet them down, but that only lasted a few instants before they were deep in conversation again. I figured, what the hell, I'll just ask what I really wanted to know.

"Does anyone know who is behind these attempts?" I asked, trying to slip it in organically.

They both stopped and stared. I don't think they thought I cared or that I was listening to their constant chatter.

"No, milady," hair lady replied. Of course, why would

they give me anything, my grandfather was probably high on the list. And now I alerted them so they would quit talking.

"You know, I've been coming for days, and I don't know what you're called?" I switched topics, trying to disarm them.

"Oh, I'm Tessa," the hair lady said.

"I'm Sencha," the make-up lady said.

"I'm Brigid," I added, so they didn't think I was stealing their names. They were only giving me the names they "went by" not their real ones, so my gift should be better received.

"That's my given name." I added so they would understand the trust I was giving them.

"That is very kind, Lady Brigid," they both said in unison. They knew not to thank anyone, which was something that even with the magic ball's power running through me I had a hard time remembering.

I inclined my head gently to them, since Tessa still had a firm grip on my hair.

"I know that people believe my grandfather is involved, but his loyalty is true. Who else do people suspect?" I asked.

They both took in a breath, shocked that I would address their unspoken beliefs so blatantly.

"Ummm, there are several possibilities, milady."

"I'm sure. My prime suspect is the Phoenix. Is he on anyone's list?" I asked point blank.

There were surprised gasps from both of the serving ladies.

"Yes, milady," Sencha answered. Then, she closed her mouth and wouldn't say anything more. Were they afraid of the Phoenix? I couldn't see Tessa's face, but Sencha looked frightened and her hand trembled when she went to smooth on my eye shadow.

I backed off. This talk could get them in trouble. Especially if they suspected I was a spy in their midst. I was an idiot. Now they wouldn't speak any court gossip around me at all. I sighed in despair, but I had other stations, and hopefully they wouldn't alert the others, slim chance, but I hoped.

I was surprised, when near the end of the hair session—Sencha had left earlier, since my makeup was done long before the elaborate hair dressing was—Tessa leaned in close and whispered conspiratorially, "The Phoenix is everyone's top choice for the assassin, but he is so dangerous, no one dares speak it. Be careful, Lady Brigid."

I gulped. That made sense. I needed to be sneakier about this. He was the most dangerous man in the court besides the king and my grandfather.

How was I going to get my info then? "Is there a code word people use to speak of him?" I asked quietly.

Her hands stilled for a moment.

"When we wish to speak of him, we use the word bird. It's silly, but it makes us feel safer."

"You are very kind to share that, Tessa," I acknowledged, and her hands returned to twisting and tugging.

"He has spies everywhere. Be careful, we are fond of you."

I felt tears well up. I had no reason to have anyone fond of me, and it touched me deeply. I felt the need to thank her, and although the magic screamed at me not too, I said quietly. "Thank you, Tessa. You have touched me."

Her hands stilled again, and I could sense her surprise behind me. "Why would you place yourself in my debt?"

she asked, her voice uneven. She might have even believed I was setting a trap.

"Because I'm in your debt for that information. It might save your king."

"I accept," she said. A zing ran through me, and I realized that those thank yous I'd been warned about were real. I now owed her a debt. I had no idea how that would play out, but it was real, and that zing was a geas upon me.

She went back to my hair, and we finished in silence.

I proceeded to my next station, being dressed, but Sencha must have warned them as they were unnaturally silent. They kept the gossip to other servants who I didn't know rather than about the king. It was fine, the meaty thing I needed to know, I was clutching to my breast with all my will.

After my lessons with the courtiers on how to address everyone and how to recognize them by rank, I transported back to my grandfather's to change and practice with Dana —the worst part of my day. The only thing that cheered me was maybe I'd be better when the final conflict with the witches happened, if I could ever go home. That sent me down the rabbit hole of worry for Gabe and what was happening back home. We'd essentially disappeared for a couple of weeks now, and everyone must be frantic or think we were dead. What was going to happen to my friends, to my house?

Dana slapped those creepy long hands at me when I drifted away in a funk. My eyes snapped back to hers, and she crisply demanded I throw the ball of electricity again. My throwing was still disappointing, and the look in her eyes let me know that was one trick unavailable in my repertoire, and thus out of hers.

"Is it true not everyone here has magic?" I asked her.

Mainly to distract her from making me do it again and again. My arm felt like it wanted to fall off.

She ignored me. "Use the other arm. You use that one constantly, and it isn't working. Aim a bolt with your left arm."

It felt awkward, but when I aimed at the target, the bolt struck true. At least it hit the target, if only barely.

We both froze in surprise.

"Hmmm, it seems you are better when you don't think too hard about it," she remarked.

It was true, I'd basically shot from the hip.

"Finally," I grumped.

"Again." she commanded. Not that I wasn't expecting that.

Each bolt erupted on the target closer and closer to the center, and the excitement in my chest grew. I could do it; I could aim lightning without killing anyone near me.

Of course, that excitement ended with a flash, when she said we were moving out of the safe room to the practice field where others would be. My knees began to shake.

"What if it doesn't work when I know it's not safe for everyone?" I asked, my voice quivering.

"Then they will die."

Like that helped.

We stood in the practice yard. I swallowed down the urge to yell, "Incoming." Mostly because Dana would probably smack me upside the head. She wanted me tense and focused.

The targets here were further away, and the archers practicing were closer than I wished they were.

"Now, Brigid, I have work to do." Her annoyed tone stabbed through me.

I flinched, but I raised my left hand and let a bolt fly. It barely hit the edge of the target, but no one was struck, and the static in the air increased.

My anxiety was buzzing when she made me do it again. This time, the bolt went off target, and someone practicing with their bow went flying. I gasped and ran over to check on them. "Sorry, so sorry!" I kept saying. But the person was only stunned and wobbled back to a bench to get their wits back.

Now, I was terrified of killing someone, but Dana wouldn't let me back down.

She commanded me again and again, until I was frazzled, but the bolts hit true. She finally gave me one terse nod and announced that we were finished. I sighed with relief and headed to the transporter room minutes before Sorcha arrived for "tea."

She'd had to wait until her shift ended, although she only had a four-hour reprieve before she was back on duty. She exited the transporter room, and I froze to see that she was only on two legs not four.

"What?" I gasped.

She sighed. "Yes, we have two forms. It's easier to do some things this way like dine with two-leggeds. Although we don't like to change since we feel more vulnerable."

She was dressed in Fae casual—basically fitted robes—still tall, built like a warrior, but now she had small breasts, and a more regular female shape. I also noticed she had bags under eyes, and her eyes were bleary with exhaustion. I was taking her from her one chance to rest. I felt bad, but this was important. More important than sleep.

Grandfather spent some time talking to her privately in his den, before Dana, Megan, Mr. Mittens, and I were invited in. Dana brought her newest, perfected prototype to demonstrate, and those of us that had experienced it watched with high interest when the bug spread its wings over Sorcha's eyes, and she experienced the wonder of a recorded video for the first time.

She gasped and flung her arm back for her weapon but stopped herself. I was impressed that her first response was to fight, rather than to run. She was well-trained.

Once Dana plucked it from her nose, we all looked on with anticipation.

"That, that was…" She had no words.

Her eyes were alight with something. Excitement? Terror? I had no idea.

"I think that could make the difference," she finally said.

"We would need your help to deploy the bugs," my grandfather added. "We need to get them into places where it would be odd for us to be seen. However, they would be places you can go easily."

"Like where?" she asked.

"Places that the Phoenix is commonly found or where he's known to meet people privately."

"I normally only see him in the public places with the king," she responded.

"Yes, but off those rooms are the private chambers. You'd only need to crack open a door and let the bug in," Grandfather said.

She looked thoughtful. "Yes, I think that can be done. How many do you have?"

We all looked at Dana.

"There are eight working prototypes."

Eight? I thought she'd only had four. I guess she was fast at this—fast and capable.

Sorcha reached her hand out for the bug that had recorded us, and Dana plunked it into her hand. She examined it up close, weighing it, measuring it with her eyes. "I believe I can smuggle in eight of these without any trouble. When?"

"Tomorrow. I can bring you the other bugs now," Dana answered.

"How do I make them work?" Sorcha asked.

"The magic is already there; they just need the command word that will start them and another to end the recording. You will need to retrieve them within a day, if you do not, the magic will cease to work, and the bugs will fall to the ground and the recordings will be lost."

"That is reasonable," Sorcha replied. For the first time in a few days, she seemed to perk up. Hope was a powerful drug.

Dana took Sorcha to her lab for the rest of the bugs, and we retired to our rooms, anxious that all would go smoothly.

Now, it was a matter of waiting. I sucked at that. Waiting made me worry, gave me time to think of everything that could go wrong, and made me dwell on Sofia, Gabe, the house, the werewolves, Brightfeather and Goch, and me. Was I going to be trapped here forever in another horrible marriage, more of a slave now than ever? I couldn't face it. I had to find a way home—a way to end this ridiculous situation. I buried my face in the pillow that wasn't mine on a bed that wasn't my glorious king-sized memory foam. Mr. Mittens was consulting with my grandfather, and Megan was resting. I had this grand Fae power, and it was nothing without my home and my friends.

After this, if it worked, I was going to throw myself on the king's mercy and get my life back. That was the only thing that kept me going. I even wondered about Sofia. What if she made it back before me? That got my heart beating fast as I wondered if Gabe would ever escape her enslavement. I fell asleep sobbing those thoughts into the foreign pillow.

The next day was the day that Sorcha was going to deploy the bugs. Dana had gifted me with another, just in case. She'd told me to activate it with Mr. Mittens's true name, Xrsrphn. I could deactivate it with Splintercat. Since I rarely said either of those words, they were good ones for me to use. I practiced with Mr. Mittens to make sure I pronounced his name correctly.

I've also given the spymaster Sofia's name, so he can search for any mention of her, Mr. Mittens announced to me.

"There's a spymaster?" I choked out.

Of course, your grandfather is a high Fae lord, and must look out for his own interests. The spymaster requires an image as well, when you have time, stop by and give him your last mental picture.

"Didn't you give him one?"

Hmpf. He said that mine was inadequate.

I could see that. I doubted cats saw the same as us two-leggeds. I smiled at him. "I will stop by, if you show me where."

Then, we all went about our usual tasks, our minds distracted with the worry that the bugs wouldn't work, or maybe worse, would. How would we convince the king without suspicion? Without letting the scary Phoenix know? Those were worries that distracted me through queen class. I watched but had zero opportunity or need to launch my bug.

I was surprised at the end of my day—I expected to return to my grandfather's—when I was instead brought to the king and into a large dining chamber. There was a long table and seated at it were many courtiers. My lungs seized for a moment when I realized I had to perform without embarrassing anyone and without getting myself or my grandfather imprisoned—or worse—for treason.

I was announced and seated at the opposite end of the table from the king. That was a relief until I realized all eyes could watch me. Then I nearly melted the makeup off my face with flop sweat.

The only thing keeping my hair from following in a river of saltwater was its elaborate braids and all the pins. The sweat ran freely down my back, however, to make everything more comfortable. I made it through the serving of the first course without error. I kept up inane and meaningless small talk to those next to me. Finally, the nervous sweat stopped, and I made the mistake of thinking that I could handle it.

That's when the fun began.

The grand doors into the chamber opened as they had to allow me to enter earlier, and my grandfather was escorted in and seated to the king's left. He was followed shortly by the man I now knew as the Phoenix.

I gasped quietly and hid it with a delicate cough. I didn't know why my grandfather was here, and judging from his ruddy complexion, he wasn't happy about it. The Phoenix had on his court face—one that said he was pleasant and slightly amused. He took his seat on the king's right. I blinked.

My heart sped up, and my mouth went dry. What was going on? Not knowing what else to do, I pretended to reach down and grab something I'd dropped. When I did so, I took the bug from my shoe, whispered, "Xrsrphn," and let it go. It rose out of my hand and disappeared from view without anyone noticing. It should now buzz around the ceiling and record until I called it back.

I fervently wished that Mr. Mittens and Megan were with me. I couldn't see this situation ending well. There were some courtly shenanigans or machinations going on behind the scenes that I didn't understand, but the level of tension in the room doubled with every course. I tried to eat, so I didn't appear rude or ungrateful, but all I could do was nibble and push things around on my plate. I couldn't hear the discussion at the other end of the table; I could only hope that the bug did.

Finally, the last course was cleared away, and we were free to exit the table to the adjoining grand throne room to mingle. My grandfather caught my eye and gestured for me to hold back and stay unnoticed.

I tried. But everywhere I went, courtiers were vying for my favor, and I had to keep up the chatter and empty compliments as I was passed from group to group. Still, I managed to keep a look out for my grandfather and the bug, which had dutifully followed us and was now lazily buzzing the ceiling of the throne room, no one the wiser. My grandfather, the king, and the Phoenix were near the throne. The Phoenix had his back to the crowd, the king facing him; my grandfather stood off to the side.

They looked to be discussing something serious. They were focused intently on each other and not paying attention to anything else. I was still being shuffled from group to group, so I couldn't keep a constant eye on them.

A scream rang out, my breath caught, my heart beat hard, and I twisted to see what was happening. The king was being hurried away by his Shadows who, until then, had been lining the walls. Others were dragging my grandfather and the phoenix away. I ran towards them. Before I'd gone more than a few steps, I was also being grabbed and wrenched back. I reached out my hand, whispered, "Splintercat," and the bug dropped into my hand. Then I was being shoved to and fro. I fell at one point and used the motion to put the bug back in my shoe. A rough hand finally hauled me up, and two of the Shadows I'd never met escorted me out—under arrest.

Chapter Twelve

My heart was in my throat, and I begged them to tell me what had happened. After they'd bound my hands with magic dampening cuffs, one smacked me across the face and said, "That's because the Pendragon tried to kill the king." She bent down closer and hissed into my ear, "You'll never replace me in his bed." I recoiled in shock and hurt.

Realization hit me with a blast. This was the leader of the Scáthanna—the king's mistress. What had Sorcha called her? I racked my brain, but nothing came to me. I was too worried about my fate. Didn't matter that I didn't want to replace her in his bed, she would have it out for me. I would be replacing her in a way. I doubted they'd end their affair over something so trite as a political marriage, but maybe he was the loyal type. I muffled a laugh in my shoulder. I was growing punchy as I was dragged and poked and prodded down a hall, out a door, and down several staircases.

We walked forever. It made sense to me in a way. Why would you want your dungeon to be under your palace? They appeared to be linked, but it felt like we walked miles, and as big as it was, the palace wasn't *this* large. We finally entered the part where the cells were kept. They weren't what I expected, no iron bars, no dirt floors or filthy people weeping and wailing. The cells were separated by clear sheets of something I'd say looked like acrylic. I knew that wasn't true, because this was a different planet with different resources.

A door opened into an empty cell. The floor was stone, and there was a cot and a wooden bucket for waste. They removed my cuffs and the king's mistress shoved me roughly inside with a sneer. I rubbed my wrists. The sensation of having my magic shut down was like having a nerve block in a way. I could feel heat, cold, and sensation, but at the same time I felt numb. It was hard to describe.

Once the door shut, I realized the numbness was gone, but when I tried to reach for my magic, it was faint and far away. Whatever the thick clear walls were, they continued to block magic. I pressed a hand against the clear door, and a shock drove me back. I rubbed my hand against the smooth fabric of the elaborate gown I wore. I looked around. Because the walls were transparent, I could see several other inmates in the dungeon. I scanned for my grandfather. Would he be brought here? Would they execute him? What was going to happen?

I hoped we had a chance to show our evidence, if we had some. The bug. I needed to see what it saw. I looked around, but the inmates were focused on their own misery, and no one was watching me. I dug the bug from my shoe, and like Dana had shown me, I placed it on the bridge of my nose. It activated its replay mode. I had to watch it in real time because it didn't have a fast forward or reverse. But it looked like time wasn't a problem for me.

Most of what I watched was cringe worthy. I looked

ridiculous trying to be a courtier. I could pull off a gown, but not as daily wear. I usually relied on jeans and t-shirts, especially since I was out of the corporate world. I pulled my attention back from me and focused on the king. There was a lot of background noise, so I couldn't tell what they were saying in the dining room. I hoped it would clear up when we switched back to the throne room.

There we went. The king led the way, followed by my grandfather and the Phoenix. I was in the last group since I'd been at the far end of the table. We were all gathered in various groups in the throne room, and the bug circled, getting video of different parts of the room. How I wished that instead of a limited magical bug, we'd had a drone to focus on what I wanted to see and hear. Again, an occasional snippet of conversation I could understand wafted through, but most was a hum of noise with only random words peering out.

There. They were in position and the bug was headed in that direction. Maybe it saw what had happened. I continued to watch, my breath ragged and my hands clenched in anticipation.

It was subtle. My grandfather turned slightly to look at something that the Phoenix was gesturing towards. When he did, his shoulders blocked the king's view, and the Phoenix used the opportunity to stab forward with a stiletto, hiding his intent and making it hard to distinguish which of the men did it.

The knife flashed towards the king and was eaten up in the king's voluminous robes. I gasped. The king lurched back, igniting a flare of magic that whited out the bug for an instant. When the flash ended, I saw my grandfather's eyes flick to the knife and reach towards the Phoenix to grab it from him. Then I couldn't see anymore because the centaurs leapt forward, and it was too chaotic. Plus, the bug had moved away. We had it. We had the proof.

I closed the bug carefully and stuck it back in my shoe. Now, how did I get it into the right hands? How did I get free long enough to save my grandfather and myself? Would any of my magic reach through these walls? Could I call Mr. Mittens?

I sat on the cot, and gingerly felt my check. It was a little swollen and now that the sting of the slap had diminished and left it throbbing. I set my mind to ignore it, and closed my eyes, intent on sending one call to my cat, my one protector in this realm now that my grandfather was arrested. I didn't know if I could depend on Sorcha, or if she would risk her neck to get us out, but I knew Mr. Mittens would do anything for me. I concentrated and yelled with all my will and intent over and over at him until I was interrupted by a jailer bringing in food. After that, I continued until I must have fallen asleep.

The next day was more of the same. They fed us two meals, and I spent the rest of the time calling to my cat. It was mentally exhausting, especially when I spent that energy on something I wasn't sure would even work. I don't know how many days I tried until I decided I had to try something else. If Mr. Mittens had heard me, he'd be here. I had to conclude that he couldn't hear me. I needed to break through the walls to give my call a chance. I tried each aspect of my magic. Water wasn't an option since I had none but what little they gave me to drink. I tried using earth to fling stones against the clear panes of the prison walls. The stones from the floor barely wobbled. I did manage between my fingers and my magic to pry one up and use it to bang against the walls. It did nothing.

Fire didn't scorch the material either. My strongest, messiest, magic was lightning, but I kept it as a last resort. It wouldn't do anyone any good if I ended up taking myself out with it. After everything else failed, I attempted to gather it in my hand. A few sparks flicked between my fingers. I'd never build significant power by going quickly. This was the last resort, if I didn't pull this together, free myself, and show the evidence, we were doomed. I'd never get home, Gabe would be enslaved forever, and my house would go back to a state of rot. I wanted to sob, only crying did nothing. I was a strong woman. I had a goal; I just had to work.

I waited until the second meal was delivered and I knew I'd have a span of uninterrupted time. The sparks were so small, I almost despaired, but I continued to layer sparks a little at a time. The sweat poured off me, but I had time—all night until the morning meal was brought—and no interruptions.

Sparks layered on top of sparks and started to stick. A tiny electric ball the size of a BB grew in my palm. I figured I had to increase it to at least the size of a softball to have any chance of it being useful against the magic walls of my cell. I kept my concentration on it for hours. I don't know how I did it, except for the fact I had to. No one else could save me. When I heard the breakfast servants coming down the stairs, I knew it was time. My electric ball wasn't quite to softball size, but it was somewhere in between a baseball and a softball, and I was out of time. If I didn't try now, I'd have to release it and try again after the evening meal when I had enough time to build it back up, and I didn't know if I could concentrate that long without sleep two nights in a row.

I stood and walked carefully to the door, keeping my concentration up and the ball crackling in my hand. I checked for the guards or for the servants bringing breakfast, but my portion of the dungeon was clear. I probably had other inmates watching me, or they continued to ignore each other as they sat in their own world of misery. I didn't have the energy to notice. I said a short prayer, applied the concentrated lightning to the mechanism in the door, and sent my will outward to push through the door to the other side. For a moment, the lightning ball sat there between my palm and the material of the door, and nothing happened. I pushed with all my might, the effort causing my arm to shake. I placed my other hand over the one with the lightning, and using my back foot continued the pressure. The lightning bucked and wiggled in my hand, trying to take off in another direction, since the wall material was resistant. I curled my fingers around it slightly. I imagined my hand sizzling under the concentrated electricity, but I set my will and kept pressing. Finally, to my relief, the ball began to melt its way through the door material, magic and all.

I'd hoped it would be an instant process. But it took several minutes. When the door finally cracked open, the magic broken, I could hear the guards approaching on their rounds. There was some commotion in my cell block, and I looked around. The other inmates had been watching me. The closest beckoned for me to come close and let them out.

I shook my head, and mouthed, "Sorry." Their plight touched me, but I couldn't help, I didn't have time. The noise of trays being scraped over floors was growing louder, and I knew the guards would turn the corner and see me at any moment. I'd done nothing but study how to get out of the dungeon in the days I'd spent trying to contact Mr. Mittens—staring at the halls and where guards and servants turned and disappeared to. I chose a corridor that seemed empty and bolted out.

Once free of the cell, my magic rushed back. I felt revived and tingling with energy, which I needed after my all-night vigil. I wrapped myself in shadow and looked around to find an exit or a good place to hide. The corridors were narrow, and I'd have to avoid guards running into me as I made my way out. It wouldn't be long until someone noticed my cell was empty, my door open, and the cell magic broken.

I didn't give myself much of a chance if they recaptured me. They'd keep me in magic dampening cuffs forever if I was caught. I tried to control my breathing, since it seemed loud and rasping to me, but the adrenaline was hard to fight when I was so afraid of getting caught. I slipped down an empty corridor and ran to the end. A dead end. This part only dropped a level to more cells. I retraced my steps. We had come down to this level, I needed to find a staircase that went up if I wanted out.

I tried another corridor. More cells, no exit. The next corridor had many guards running about. The alarm had been sounded, at least I could hear guards yelling that there was an escape. Now, they were actively looking for me. This had to be the one that led to the exit. Even though they couldn't see me, I could easily bump into someone if I wasn't careful and give myself away. The gown I still wore wasn't helping. It was voluminous and would get in the way. I stripped down to my underwear. For a gown like this, they had me in a type of shift. It had support for my breasts and hugged my form to mid-thigh where it flared into a short skirt. I reminded myself no one could see me as I kicked the gown as far as possible into a corner. I renewed my shadow camouflage, checked the busy corridor, and rushed in between the masses of people, avoiding touching anyone as best as I could.

I only bumped into one person, but they blamed a guard next to them. I cleared the last corner, and the exit to the prison became visible. My heart thumped in my throat, and my breath was ragged. I raced to the exit.

"Mr. Mittens!" I yelled mentally.

I could feel his surprise. *Brigid? Where are you? What happened?* his mental voice rang between my ears, filling me with happiness.

I looked around, the coast was still clear, and I bolted to the door. "I've been in the dungeon, locked up. I'm escaping now." I hoped, anyway.

I'm coming.

I nearly sobbed in relief. I ripped the door open. There were more guards outside the door, and I almost backpedaled, but I knew they couldn't see me, although the door opening on its own had to be suspicious. I hoped Faerie had ghosts, and the guards were superstitious.

They weren't, dammit. The door opening alerted them, and they branched out, completely aware that someone masked from their view was here. I stopped suddenly when one of the guards told everyone to be quiet and listen for the intruder. I was wearing soft court shoes, but all the marble-like flooring made even a soft shoe loud.

We were at an impasse. All of us were still and listening. I just hoped my panicked breathing didn't give me away, so I worked at taking small shallow breaths and tried to calm my racing heart.

Where was my cat? How long would it take him to find

me? Did I need to call him to me and hope my inherent magic would bring him, or would it hurt him to be hurtled through space at me? I didn't dare. I had to wait. I also had to remember he was in trouble with the court and had been banished to Earth. I didn't want him hurt or killed either. But, he could realm walk, and I hoped if he were in trouble, he'd escape.

There was a loud clatter behind the guards, their heads turned, and I used the noise to skitter forward. More rattles and clanks—it sounded like armor. Were more guards on their way? I had to use the noise to flee, so I scurried forward a few more steps and waited for more noise. It came, I fled to the doorway and through—expecting to see rows of soldiers on the other side. Nothing.

Chapter Thirteen

I looked around. Up ahead, Mr. Mittens in his Splintercat form turned a corner dragging a long chain. He stopped briefly and rattled it. I wanted to scream his name and gather him in my arms and squeeze the stuffing out of him.

Instead, I sent him a mental, "I'm in front of you."

We should run, pet, he replied.

I ran. I skidded around the corner with Mr. Mittens. He could easily outpace me, but he heard me just fine and stayed by me. I wrapped him in shadow as we went, although the passage of the air kept wearing our camouflage away, and I had to concentrate to keep us hidden.

I didn't know where to go or how to get my evidence to the king. The only person I could think of was Sorcha. I wondered if being my escort had resulted in her also being imprisoned. I hadn't spent time looking in the cells during my desperate escape from the dungeon. Although, I'd like to think I'd have noticed her if she were there.

"Mr. Mittens," I gasped as I ran, "We need to find Sorcha. Any ideas?"

I'm a cat making a jail break. That's the extent of my plans, he mumbled.

Fair enough. "Where are the *Baincapall?* You must have seen some on your way in," I insisted.

I did see some heading into the palace, but I don't know where they went.

Nope, that made sense, they must have been called in to guard the king. I had to think. Where would the king be? It was daylight, shouldn't he be holding court in the throne room? My thoughts raced even as my legs faltered. I was worn down and exhausted. I couldn't keep up this pace. "Stop for a minute," I begged my cat.

My shadow magic was thin, so I watched as he looked around and found an alcove. We ducked in, breathing hard, and I renewed the shadow magic hiding us. "I think we're going to have to find the throne room and get the bug to Sorcha. I only hope she's there."

All the guards are searching for you. Do you think that is a good idea? Mr. Mittens's sarcastic voice rang through my head.

"No, but I have to prove our innocence, and to do that, the king has to see the recording on this bug."

Hmpf.

His weight slumped against me, and I staggered as my hand reached out on its own to stroke his silky fur. A different sensation from his Ragdoll floof.

We have to retrace some of our path, pet. I can already hear guards coming this way. Are you sure? He shifted and the weight against my leg went away.

I nodded, then remembered he couldn't see me. Truth was I wasn't sure, but I saw no other way out of the mess if the king didn't get the evidence. "Yes."

Fine. The coast is clear, let's go. His mental voice was resigned.

I slipped out of the alcove and looked both ways; it was clear. We retraced our steps. I knew I was close to him because his fur brushed my hand. I was grateful for the small comfort it brought me. If Mr. Mittens were here, I was safe. He would kill anything that threatened me. I was sure of it. We slunk down the corridor and passed several courtiers, servants, and guards. The guards grew thicker the closer we moved to the throne room.

As we drew nearer, it was clear why we hadn't seen any *Baincapall*; they were all here ready to protect the king from me. Stupid. I wasn't a threat. The room was tightly watched, and no one was moving in or out of it. That was a problem. I searched the centaur-like guards for Sorcha, but I didn't spot her. She must be inside.

We watched for several minutes, and in that time, the doors did not open. All we could do was watch and wait.

It seemed like forever before the door opened, and when it did, it was to disgorge several courtiers. We rushed in before the door shut completely. Mr. Mittens staying close to my side.

There is your Baincapall friend, he announced before we were all the way in, and I scanned for her. His senses were more advanced than mine, and I was grateful for the reassurance she was here. I spotted her, and we made our way carefully through courtiers and servants until we were close enough she could hear me.

The constant hum and drone of voices and people moving about filled my ears, and I hoped it was enough to cover my voice this close to the warrior.

"Sorcha, don't react," I said.

She jumped slightly, but her face stayed neutral, and when I looked around, it appeared that no one noticed. Even being startled, her discipline was topnotch.

"It's Brigid. I'm cloaked. I have evidence that proves my grandfather did not try to kill the king."

Her eyes moved from side to side, trying to gauge whether or not her fellow *Baincapall* noticed the disembodied voice or not.

"What do you have?" she hissed quietly.

"A bug of the event," I answered.

"Hmmm." Her eyes continued to move side to side as she scanned the room. "This is going to be tricky. My captain hates you and will do anything to block this. I don't know how to give this evidence to the king without going through her. How good is it?" she whispered.

"It shows the event and proves that the Phoenix was the one with the knife."

"The king was injured, and the only people that have been to see him are my captain and his personal physician."

I looked over at the dais, I hadn't noticed before because of the crowds, but the throne was empty. My heart sped up further, which I didn't think was possible in the situation. I could feel panic licking the edges of my senses, as my vision narrowed, and my brain began to go haywire.

"It's got to be possible for him to see this, doesn't she want him to be safe? He's keeping the viper and blocking the mongoose."

She looked confused. Right, earth metaphors. "A viper is a venomous, oh never mind."

"I understand. Give me the bug. I'll figure it out."

I bent over to retrieve it from my shoe, when there was a bunch of rustling, and the crowd stirred. A richly dressed servant entered and walked up to the dais. He turned and stood in front of the empty throne. I stood up straight, bug forgotten for a moment.

He cleared his throat and tapped three times on the

floor with a staff to get our attention. Once he had it, the background noise died, and Mr. Mittens and I slipped behind Sorcha, since people began to move and readjust to hear the announcement.

"Hear ye, my fine courtiers." He paused for affect, making sure all eyes were on him. "Welcome back to court the Conqueror of Winter, the Subjugator of Summer, the Annihilator of Autumn, and the Vanquisher of Spring." He swept his arms around and finished. "I present to you, the High King of All Faerie!"

I could hear gasps, and the courtiers and servants all started to whisper their gossip and suppositions around the room.

"Sorcha," I whispered. "This is our chance. Do you think you can approach the king?"

She shook her head quickly, the movement slight.

"I can maybe keep my fellow Scáthanna away for a few moments if you can get near him."

I shook, and my knees went weak. Could I do this? Could I approach the king, put the bug on his nose, and get him to watch long enough that I could save my grandfather and myself? Could I do it fast enough that a *Baincapall* Scáthanna wouldn't slip a spear between my ribs?

"Mr. Mittens. Can we do this?"

He pressed against my leg, and I wobbled slightly from the force.

I will help your Baincapall friend to keep the rest at bay. Drop the shadows on my command, he replied simply.

I took a deep breath, and with my hand in his fur, we began to wend our way slowly to the dais.

The king was being escorted in by my rival, Sorcha's boss. There was a group of six other two-legged soldiers with her. They kept the king surrounded and waited until he was seated on his throne. Then the guards backed up to a position behind the throne where his guards usually waited.

We bumped into a few people, but luckily it was crowded enough that they would throw their nasty glances at someone near them and didn't suspect that invisible creatures walked among them.

It seemed like miles to reach the king. Every step felt like it was in deep sand. I panted and sweated through every step. It was a wonder the people in the room couldn't smell me. Luckily, the penchant for heavy robes meant mine wasn't the only sweaty body in the room. My trepidation and doubt grew with every step. If I failed, it could mean death for me, my cat, and my grandfather. Every footfall dragged us closer to that possible end. The room was large, but it wasn't that large, and my concentration was all about winding through the crowd, until suddenly, we were in front of the king. I halted, and Mr. Mittens did as well.

What is your plan, pet? he asked.

I didn't have one beyond "get to the king," and here we were. I thought back to him, *"Umm, go up there, plunk the bug on his nose, and hope for the best."*

That's what I was afraid of. His kitty sigh echoed between my ears. *Follow my lead and drop your shadow concealment when I tell you, come, we are going up to the throne.*

I was partly relieved he would take the lead, and of course, terrified not to be in control of the situation. But I knew this was it. We'd either succeed or die. I took a firm grip of his fur and let him lead me up the dais and into the position he wanted me.

When we were close, he spoke to the king, mind to mind. I assumed he kept his mental voice to a tight band, including only me and the king because no one else reacted to his words.

You have been greatly deceived, sire. I bring you proof of a great wrong and evidence of the true assassin that keeps attempting to end your life.

"How dare you try to tempt your king, show yourself!" the king roared.

That got everyone's attention, and the guards began to move towards us.

Now, Brigid, let the shadows fall.

I said a quick prayer to any god that could hear me and let our concealment fall. We stood before the court—me in my Fae underwear, my prison dishevelment, and stink and Mr. Mittens in all his Splintercat glory. He was poised behind the throne, his massive body between the guards and the king and a paw with knife-like claws near the king's throat. My heart leaped in my chest. This was his plan?

Brigid, his voice was calm and controlled. *Bring the bug.* I leaned down to pluck it from my shoe.

Meanwhile, his mental voice was broadcast to all in the room. *If one person takes a single step towards us, the king will die. If you wait until we are done, we will leave, and the king will be unharmed.*

I took the bug and moved towards the king. "Sire, we wish only to present this evidence. This wondrous device will show you the truth." I placed it on the bridge of his nose, and the inner wings of the beetle opened over his eyes. I knew when the recording began, because his body jerked back in his chair, and then the wonder spread over his face as the moving pictures started.

"This is miraculous," he murmured.

The guard's faces around us were murderous, and I knew that we would be harshly punished or killed on the spot if the king did not react how we wished him to. Poor Mr. Mittens was going to be banished forever from Faerie for his stunt. I guess if things didn't go our way, our best bet was to kill the king and try to flee.

The recording lasted several minutes, and the entire court seemed to hold its breath as the impasse between us and the king's guards continued.

Finally, as I watched the king's face, I saw his realization about the deception. His face flushed, and anger radiated from him. I knew the recording was near its end, and I reached over to pluck the bug from his face. Once I did, its wings closed, and I slipped the thing back into my shoe.

The king was silent. Then his head turned to gaze at Mr. Mittens. "We will have words, cat. Remove your paw from my throat."

Mr. Mittens lowered his claws and shifted back to Ragdoll form. The guards leapt forward, weapons leveled on us.

I closed my eyes and waited to feel a spear thrust between my ribs. When it didn't happen, I opened my eyes.

The king held up a hand to tell them to hold. The breath I'd been holding escaped me, and my knees finally gave way. I sank to the dais. Mr. Mittens joined me, and we sat below the king awaiting his judgment.

He called the Scáthanna leader to him. She was his mistress, and I was sure that was the end of our lives. She bent to his mouth, and he said something we couldn't hear. She jerked up sharply, pointed to a few of her soldiers, and they exited the room.

The king stood and paced back and forth for a moment, probably gathering his wits about him over the surprise we'd gifted him.

"Brigid."

I jumped, surprised he'd used my name, but then again we were engaged. Sort of. Probably not anymore. I didn't know what had happened while I was in the dungeon, but there had to be some sort of announcement.

"What was that wondrous device?"

I stood awkwardly and curtsied, Mr. Mittens small form solid next to me.

"It is a magical device that records what is happening and replays it. What you saw was exactly what happened that day, sire."

His head dipped, and his chin rested on his chest for several moments. I was still shaking and weak from the aftereffects of adrenaline. If Mr. Mittens hadn't been pressed against my leg, I'd probably sink back down to the dais.

It felt like forever, and the king stayed in that position. I could almost feel the wheels turning in his mind as he considered all that had been presented.

Finally, the main doors opened, and the guards came through, dragging the Phoenix in his court splendor, and my grandfather, who was filthy in chains and rags. His body was covered in wounds, and it was clear he'd been tortured. He stumbled and dragged one leg. My heart cried out to see him like this—a proud warrior reduced to a shadow of himself.

Warm tears ran down my cheeks. I wiped them away angrily.

The guards roughly stood both men before the king, who looked up and stared at both of them for a moment. Then he stood.

"Lugh, come forward," he ordered.

The guards dragged him to the dais and dropped him there. The chains jangled, and I could see the wounds they left on his flesh. They had to be iron. Luckily, I could see the fight was still in his eyes, as he lifted himself by sheer willpower and stood, swaying, before the king.

"Sire." A single word, but proof that he was the king's man always.

The king wasted no time. "Describe what happened the day I was stabbed."

My grandfather stared at the king, and his gaze flicked quickly to me and back.

"The Phoenix and I were engaged in conversation with you, sire. While I turned away to look for the noise that had bothered you, the Phoenix stabbed you in such a way that both of our views were blocked, and it appeared as if the knife was wielded by me. It was not true, sire."

The king called the Phoenix forward. "How would you describe the event?" he asked, all formality gone.

The Phoenix bowed elaborately. "The Pendragon speaks true for part of it." He gestured grandly to my grandfather, a smirk on his perfect face. "He was the one that stabbed you and used his movements to make it hard to distinguish between us. You arrested the right Fae." His smug demeanor made me wish *I* had a knife.

The king appeared to consider both men. I felt nervous. Would he accept the evidence we'd given him? Would he continue to harass and imprison my grandfather, or worse? My mouth was dry, but my palms were sweaty. I wiped them down my soiled shift.

The king addressed the court. "Friends and courtiers. It appears we have two conflicting accounts of the violent act upon my body. Which is the truth? You have all seen the wondrous device that the granddaughter of my Pendragon has placed upon my face, but you did not see what I have seen. The device r-records..." He looked at me when he stumbled over the foreign words.

I nodded in encouragement that he'd used the correct word.

"...Events as they occur. It paints tiny, moving pictures as they happen and lets you view them again. I have watched such a thing of the day when I was violated before you. I know the truth."

For the first time, the Phoenix looked worried. At least the smirk was gone, and a tiny line appeared between his eyes.

My grandfather only stood still and waited.

"Who, you may ask, is a loyal servant, and who is a traitor in our midst?" He looked over both of the men, and a delicious shiver ran through me. Anticipation.

"The Fae lord that stabbed me, I thought of as a true servant of the crown, even a friend, but he was ambitious and wanted my crown for himself." He faced the Phoenix. "I hereby strip you of all of your lands and titles and condemn you to death. Guards." He pointed at the Phoenix, and the guards leapt to grab him. There was a scuffle, and the Phoenix pulled another fearsome looking dagger from his robes. Before they could stop him, he threw it at the king.

The entire court held its breath, the drama unfolding in a way they never thought they'd be allowed to see. The dagger spun through the air like the tight spiral on a football. I had no idea how you threw one to get a motion like that. I assumed they would tumble end over end. Must be a magic that the Phoenix wielded. The king stumbled back but couldn't get out of the way. The dagger flew at his heart, and the king knew it.

My grandfather, wounded, exhausted, and betrayed as he was, exploded into motion. He threw himself in the path of the dagger, and it struck him in the back somewhere by his right shoulder blade. I cried out, and the court let out its collective breath. I raced to my grandfather. The king had fallen back on the dais, and I saw him reaching for his chest where the knife was headed before he realized what had happened.

His personal servants raced over but were beaten back by the guards who quickly surrounded him and protected him with their bodies. The remainder grabbed the ex-Phoenix roughly and dragged him away. He protested loudly, repeating, "I'm the rightful King, kill the traitor!" But no one listened, and finally as the door shut behind him, I heard sobbing and pleading.

I sat by my grandfather and cradled his head in my hands. Mr. Mittens stared at him as though the power of his gaze would heal him. No one was paying attention to us, so I whispered, "Get Dana, please!"

Mr. Mittens blinked; his gaze caught by the sight of my grandfather bleeding on the floor. But then he took one step and disappeared before my eyes. I felt the pulse of power and realized he'd realm walked. I didn't know how that worked, but as long as it did, I was thrilled.

Chapter Fourteen

My grandfather and I were ignored as the king was hurried away to safety. From what, when the danger was gone, I didn't know, probably just a part of the court protocol.

It felt like hours but couldn't have been more than minutes before Mr. Mittens reappeared, running with Dana through the doors into the room. I'd been keeping pressure on the wound as best I could with the knife still stuck in his back. The tension in my body eased some at seeing Dana. I didn't trust her fully, but for this I did. I didn't know her agenda, but I was sure she was loyal to my grandfather. Tears started to fall as she rushed to us.

Her face, strange as it was, had a perfect human expression of despair on it. She loved him, I realized. That was the source of her loyalty. She knelt down by me and held her hand over the knife and the wound. She pulled something from a bag slung over her head and shoulder, and with her other hand, removed the knife quickly. My grandfather gasped and bright blood burbled and foamed out of the wound. Blood poured from his mouth and nose. It must have hit his lung.

Dana used the knife to cut his clothes away and pressed whatever she'd taken from her bag to the wound. My grandfather coughed, and more blood sprayed from his mouth. I sobbed silently.

She muttered something and pulled something else from the bag, one of her magical balls. This one was mottled and ugly. She handed it to me.

"Get him to swallow this."

I wasn't able to say anything back, but I turned his head and slid my fingers between his lips, "You have to swallow this, grandfather, to get better." I wasn't sure if he heard me, but his mouth was slack, and I pushed it to the back of his tongue. Nothing happened. "Swallow," I commanded louder and pressed his mouth closed. His eyes flickered open and then closed, but he swallowed. I used the hem of my ruined shift to wipe his mouth and nose clear of blood. He was limp, and there was so much blood. Dana continued to work on the wound, and finally, I saw it start to close.

My grandfather's breathing seemed to ease some, and the blood stopped. I breathed a sigh of relief. Dana sat back on her haunches, and the tension left her shoulders. She also looked relieved. I looked into her face.

"He's going to be fine," she said without my asking.

"Thank you," I said. I didn't care about the debt that would incur. I truly owed her.

She gave me a brief nod. Really, just a short bob of her head.

Now that I wasn't focused on just my grandfather, I realized Mr. Mittens had been by my side the whole time, I reached out a hand and stroked his head. "Thank you, too.

He wouldn't have made it without your quick actions." No debt was incurred thanking my non-Fae cat, but I owed him one, too. He leaned against me, and his purr soaked through and eased the rest of the tension.

"Is it safe to take him home?" I asked Dana.

"He should be able to walk in a few minutes, then it would be best if he rested."

"Can he walk all the way to the transporter room?"

"With help, we'll get him there."

"OK."

We waited until he indicated he wanted to try to stand. Just before we attempted to get him into standing position, a group of people came through the doors and hurried towards us. They looked like servants or courtiers. At least they were well dressed and officious looking.

They stopped before us at the bottom of the dais. A pompous looking Fae in rich, voluminous robes addressed us. "I'm here at the king's behest. I'm the king's personal physician and at your service." He looked as though butter wouldn't melt in his mouth, and although he was below us, I had the impression he was looking down his nose at us.

If it hadn't been for Dana, my grandfather would be dead. I wasn't that impressed with the king's physician. He'd taken his sweet time getting here, I was positive, and I had a hard time keeping the disdain from my voice. "You're a little late. We're good. Scurry off to your master."

Mr. Mittens's purr stuttered, and Dana gave a soft gasp. I'd probably pissed off the wrong dude again, but I refused to care. We helped my grandfather to his feet, and between the two of us, supported him so he could stumble to the transporter room. Once we were at the bottom of the dais, the physician's group simply moved out of the way. The court, who had stayed to watch the drama, watched us although no one ran over to help. Even bent over, supporting half of my grandfather's weight, I kept my gaze up, eyes glaring their way. Most averted their eyes from the accusation and disdain in mine. The physician's face was red with fury, but he too shifted out of our way. Mr. Mittens galloped in front of us, transforming from Ragdoll to Splintercat form, and people scurried away faster.

Mr. Mittens used his hard head to shove the doors open, and we followed all the way to the transporter room—people backing away from the fierce cat, us, and the wounded general.

───

My grandfather had been very near death, and even with Dana's magical healing ability and medicines, he still needed a few days rest in bed to recover fully. I kept expecting soldiers or *Baincapall* to show up at the gates and haul us all back to prison, but nothing of the sort happened. On the third day, Grandfather was back in his den, although slow and not completely himself. He sat by the fire, fully dressed, and summoned us in.

The three of us entered and sat with him by the fire.

He was silent for several long moments, then he simply said, "Thank you."

Since that was not normal for the Fae and would incur a debt, I accepted his thanks, but rose and threw my arms around his neck. "I couldn't bear to lose you, too," I said simply, and was surprised when his arms wrapped around me as he returned the hug.

After a while, I released him, and he let me go.

"I've had word from the king. He's coming here."

My head swam. What new hell was this? I must have blanched, because my grandfather smiled gently. "Don't worry."

"Don't worry?" I heard Megan repeat. "They've already thrown both of you in prison, and you almost died!" She paced a circle and came back to continue her tirade. "They kept us locked in this castle, and I couldn't…" she looked at me and trailed off. "Do anything." She finished eyes down, shoulders slumped.

Since Megan had covered it all, I huffed out a lame, "Yeah, that."

My grandfather chuckled, obviously not worried. "I believe this will be a pleasant visit. The king is in our debt."

I narrowed my eyes at him, attempting to read his body language. He appeared relaxed. "You're sure?"

He gave me that Fae single bob of the head that was more an acknowledgement than a yes. He looked us over. "You should go dress to welcome the king."

We were dressed in Fae casual—robes made of the iridescent silky material that on earth would be formal, our hair down in the everyday style here.

"I'm done impressing him. I'm not changing."

Megan simply stood next to me, arms crossed. Mr. Mittens stayed splooting in front of the fire, his eyes drifting between the three of us.

"As you desire," Grandfather said, but his eyes narrowed, and he looked uncomfortable.

Too bad. I was done with all the nonsense. If that kept the king from wanting to marry me, or offended him, screw 'im. My hand dropped to my side, and Megan grasped it. I squeezed hers and went to sit down and await whatever new nonsense the king brought with him.

As we waited in silence, servants entered and left, turning the den into a welcoming room with refreshments. Finally, the king was announced, and he and two Scáthanna entered the room, flanking him on both sides—the mistress, I still couldn't remember her title, and Sorcha. I smiled at my friend, and although she fought it, her lips lifted a tiny bit at the corners.

They checked the room and then retreated to the doors to make sure no one could enter without being checked by them. The king was offered a seat facing my grandfather, and the rest of us stood behind my grandfather's chair.

We waited for the king to speak. He took his sweet time, probably hunting for words.

"Lugh, I must apologize for treating you the way I did," the king began.

I almost fell over from shock. This was a lot more straightforward than I thought he would be.

"I've ever been loyal to you, sire," Lugh replied.

The king looked at the fire. He looked for all the world as though he was ashamed—as he should, in my opinion.

"I shouldn't have doubted that. You have proven your loyalty again and again, but I allowed the worm of suspicion to crawl in my ear on the voice of my Phoenix."

There wasn't an answer to that, so we all remained silent.

"I can't make up for what I did to you and your great-granddaughter, but I can offer something as a token of my faith in you." I blinked, and my grandfather folded his hands in his lap, looking down.

"My loyalty isn't something that can be bought. It lies in the faith I have in you as a ruler," my grandfather said.

"This isn't to buy your loyalty, but to show that I know of it, and am grateful for it," the king replied.

There was some political game going on. I didn't get it or want anything to do with it. However, my grandfather seemed to know how to play. So, I continued to watch and didn't interfere or storm out. Megan and Mr. Mittens watched me to see what I would do, and when I didn't react, they relaxed.

"I'm raising you from Pendragon to Phoenix," the king continued.

My grandfather stiffened. "I wish you wouldn't. I'm much better at leading armies than politics."

The king smiled. I thought he'd be angry, but he appeared to expect that response. "I think you've always been good at politics, you are just terrible at kowtowing."

Grandfather laughed. "True."

"This is temporary." The king waved away my grandfather's concerns. "I want you to find your replacement. We both know you are much better at leading my armies and fighting my wars than you are at court. But it's time to scare the rest of the traitors into the light once and for all. Would you do this for me?" he asked.

My grandfather tilted his head and looked at the king. "I will."

"Good, it's settled." He stood and brushed his hands down his thighs as though to wipe away sweat. The king worried, huh?

"Before we partake of those lovely refreshments, there's one more thing." He looked at me. "Brigid."

I jumped.

"Yes, sire." My voice squeaked a little, and I cleared my throat.

"I owe you a boon."

"A boon, sire?" I repeated, confused.

"Ask me for anything within my power, and I will grant it."

I looked at my friends and my grandfather, but their faces gave me nothing. I cleared my throat again, nervously. "There is only one thing I want, sire."

"Ask," he repeated.

"I want to go home to Earth. I'd like to be able to visit my grandfather, and he me without issue." I attempted to read his face and his posture, but it gave me nothing. "There's one more thing. I do not wish to marry you. I have someone back on Earth." I fidgeted, nervous I would offend him. "I don't wish to offend, sire, you seem lovely, but I have a life I want to go back to, and that life isn't here."

The king was quiet, contemplative. "Granted."

I nearly dropped to the floor in relief. "If I may be so bold, sire."

"Yes." This time he frowned. I probably was starting to piss him off.

"The *Baincapall* captain loves you. If you must marry, choose the one that makes you happy."

He sighed, and his eyes flicked to her standing at the door. He inclined his head at me but didn't say anything else. He went to the table, chose some refreshments, and ate. We followed. Not much conversation passed, all of us deep in our own minds, but near the end the mood changed, and soon we were all chatting meaninglessly. Soon enough, the king and his entourage left.

"We can go home!" I said to Megan and Mr. Mittens.

"Finally!" Megan crowed happily, and even Mr. Mittens's face was less grumpy for a while.

My grandfather was happy for us, but he seemed sad. Since I was on a roll, before we left the room and went to our rooms for the night, I left him with this thought.

"Dana is in love with you."

He looked like a man that had been hit upside the head with a two by four.

"What?"

I grinned and followed Megan and Mr. Mittens out and left him to figure it out by himself.

Chapter Fifteen

Dana thought she could teach me how to realm walk back home—without stripping my magic away again—quickly. If she wasn't able to, we'd have to wait for my grandfather to take us, and he was tied up with his new court business, without a timeline. Dana couldn't take a passenger, and neither could Mr. Mittens, so it was me or an indefinite waiting period for my grandfather. Now that I knew I could go back and everything here was fixed, I was desperate to do so.

There was one more issue. I needed to know about Sofia. With all the other things going on, like prison, I hadn't been free to investigate her or see if she'd survived after her failed marriage proposal to the king. I'd never visited the spymaster to give my description, since I ended up in the dungeon before I could.

Communication and news sources weren't the same here as on earth. There wasn't a widespread network that didn't involve spies and magic.

I finally went in and gave a detailed description of what

she looked like and her capabilities to the spy network. They were already keeping her on their watch list, so my input had been minor to zero on the help scale. After it was done, I did have to fight my desire to check every three minutes, even though that was ridiculous.

Then, because I needed something to do in the meantime, I continued with my magic lessons. I'd been declared "adequate" in water, fire, earth, shadow, and light. I considered Dana's "adequate" to be high praise, considering the source. I felt adept at those magics. She thought I was "fair" at lightning but wasn't willing to practice it now that my grandfather didn't require it for his failed plan that we'd never had a chance to put into action. I didn't blame her. It scared me, too.

I had realm walking to figure out, and I was finally going to learn what aether was and how to use my time magic.

Mind was telepathy, and since I was using that already with the non-speaking creatures in my midst, Dana wasn't motivated to teach me more. Since the other thing it did was give me the ability to exert mind control over others, she wasn't willing to participate as my guinea pig. Because that particular power made me feel icky, I didn't push it. Spirit did have to do with ghosts, but it was a passive power, only giving me the ability to see and hear them, which did not require training.

I was anxious to begin. I wanted to finish and take us all home as soon as possible. Dana gave me one of her patented dark looks when the first thing out of my mouth was, "What is Aether?" That question had been eating at me for a while. I mean, I knew that it was once considered the stuff that made up the heavens, but that meant *nothing* to me in terms of my magic.

She gave me a look that lasted longer than was comfortable before she answered, "Aether is the ability to connect to the spiritual and the power of intuition." That meant nothing to me.

"I don't know what that means," I said, bluntly.

She sighed. Her look was one that showed how hard it was to work with someone as ignorant as me. "Once trained, you should be able to foresee certain happenings."

"Like tell the future?"

She inclined her head. "More or less."

"How much training does it require?" I continued to badger her.

"Much, and you'll need another teacher, it is not a skill of mine."

I shrugged. I didn't want to know the future. I barely had the mental fortitude to deal with the present. "No worries."

She started with the problems of realm walking, namely the one I discovered on my own—stripping my magic away accidentally.

"How do you protect yourself from that?" I asked.

She frowned since I'd interrupted her. "You create a mental shield. It is difficult at first, but it will become automatic the more you practice."

The next issue was not *walking* into a solid structure. I shuddered at that one. When I'd *walked* us that first time, I hadn't known any of this, in fact I hadn't even intended to bring us anywhere else, it was blind luck I hadn't implanted us all in a tree. We'd ended up in a forest after all.

Before she'd let me explore any realm walking, I had to practice a mental shield. It had the added benefit of keeping me safe from others with mind magic. Once I had it down, no one weaker than me would be able to enter my mind, read my thoughts, or control me. She had me visualize a rock wall around my thoughts. I tried, but each time she launched an attack at me, my wall fell. After the fifth attempt, I was growing tired, and she was becoming more irritated.

"Children learn this quicker," she snapped at me.

I didn't know why I wasn't getting it. The concept was easy, I could build the wall in my thoughts, I just couldn't maintain the necessary concentration. The second she sent any level of mental assault, the wall disappeared.

This had to be from my years as Evan's emotional whipping post. I was used to crumbling and giving up just to keep the peace. I had to get over this. I'd gotten over him— I'd stood up to him, left him, divorced him. This should be easy, I'd already conquered it, even though it wasn't a mental attack such as Dana was using. In the past, I'd learned how to bend, not block, Evan's attacks. Maybe that was my issue. I had to let the mental attacks bend around me, rather than blocking them.

I had her try again, and I imagined the attack was one of Evan's verbal assaults about how I looked. "Are you going to lose weight? Why did you do your hair like that? Are you wearing that to the party?" Then, I did my usual thing of letting them wash over me so I could avoid the hurt, the underlying insults, and the pure nastiness he'd thrown in every statement or question.

I could feel Dana's mental assaults bend around me. They didn't bounce off or stop at a wall as she'd described. Instead, they just bent and went on by. After several moments, she stopped and stared at me.

"That should not work," Dana said, a deep frown on her horsey face.

I looked at her. "Why not?"

"That is not how it is done."

"It's how I do it," I countered.

"Hmm. Let's try again."

I could feel her attack increase in intensity, and again, I imagined myself as a stone in the river and the attack the water. I let it warp around me rather than batter me.

"I don't know how that will protect you from depleting your magic when you *walk*," she said. I realized it wasn't a frown, since it was hard to read her non-human face, but confusion.

I wasn't worried. I knew nothing would get through my defense. I'd used this for years, and now that I knew it was a shield, I realized I was well practiced.

"It'll work," I said simply.

"Well, we will know as soon as we practice," she stated haughtily.

"Yeah, I guess so. Are we doing that soon?"

She stared at me, her shark eyes unblinking. "Yes."

A mixture of excitement and terror filled me, and I felt nauseous. "OK."

"What does this, 'OK' mean? You speak it often," she asked.

I thought. I knew what it meant, but I had no idea where it had come from. It was an old expression. "It means that everything is alright. It's good."

"I see."

"So, are we going to go home, to Earth I mean?" My stomach rolled over, and I thought I'd throw up.

"We are not ready for that. I will take you to the place all realm walkers from Faerie go to practice. There won't be a spot to walk into terrain, dangerous animals, creatures, or people. It is as safe a place as we can go."

I was disappointed and a little relieved, but I nodded. I

had to learn how to avoid landing myself or my friends in something solid, so that made sense.

"O…um, alright. I'm ready."

She gave me a sidelong glance. It mainly said, "You are an idiot." I knew I wasn't actually ready, I just wanted to try and master this as soon as possible.

"How do I activate the magic and tell it where to go?" I asked.

"You are ready, but you don't know?" she asked sarcastically.

I sighed. "I know I was a bit premature. I'm ready to learn and practice."

"That's better." She handed me one of her magic balls. I didn't know what it was for, so I just stood there, my hand outstretched, the purplish ball lying in my palm.

"This is a precaution. As long as it stays in your hand, if we encounter any issues, it will snap you back to this spot. Among other things."

I stared at it; glad I didn't have to swallow it. It was bigger than the marble sized ones I was familiar with. More of a golf ball, and if I had to swallow it, I was doomed. I'd choke and die for sure.

"Now, I'm going to give you a mental picture, so don't block me. This is the training site."

I was careful to let her in, so I knew where we were going. It felt strange, having someone in my mind, forcing an image there, like cold fingers grabbing my brain. I struggled with not pushing her out. I knew I was successful when the image appeared. It was a grassy field, with what looked like a fence in the distance as well as some low outbuildings. I nodded once I had the image firmly in my mind.

"Before you ask your magic to transport you, don't

forget to bring up your shield. I'll follow, so don't try to come back until I am there. Hold that ball tightly."

I clasped my fingers around it until I knew it was secure. I concentrated on my shield and let everything pass by. Once I had that firm, I pictured the place she had shown me, felt the connection to my magic, and stepped forward.

Chapter Sixteen

I must have closed my eyes because when I opened them, I was in the grassy field. It was so earth-like, that for a moment, I thought I had traveled to Earth, and joy filled me. Dana arrived a second after, and her nod let me know I'd done well.

Moments later, I knew this was not earth. The air smelled odd. Not bad, just not like home. It wasn't as rich as Faerie either, so I knew we were on a different world. I wanted to jump up and down, but Dana wanted to test my magic to make sure my shield had worked.

She had me call light, and soon a small ball of glittering diamond sat in the palm opposite the one with the purplish ball. I did a little victory dance.

"It worked! I did it!"

"Hmmm." She looked serious, then she smiled a little. "Now, go back. I'll see if you can remember all the steps."

I frowned. A dark shadow fell over me. Since it had been a bright sunny day on whatever world this was, I looked up in curiosity. Something was flying over us. Not a vehicle that I knew of, but something large like Goch. It wasn't a dragon though. I looked at Dana. She glanced up as well, and then lunged at me, and we fell to the ground. The magic ball flew out of my hand.

A blast of wind flung my hair around and tugged at my clothing. "What's going on?" I yelled at Dana over the rush of air.

"It's a hunter," she explained.

I didn't know what that meant to her. I knew what a hunter did, they hunted and killed. So, I caught her meaning and her fear. "I thought you said this planet is safe."

"It is for realm walking. We don't ever stay here, and we rarely run into the natural predators."

"Great, just great. What now?"

"Go back. You do remember how?" she sneered.

I did. But I needed the magic ball to ensure I did it safely. I looked forward for it. The grass kept its secrets. I scrambled forward and skimmed my hands through the base of the grass stalks, searching and feeling for the ball.

"What are you doing?" Dana hissed. "It'll be back soon!"

"I dropped the ball!" I hissed back.

"Incompetent!"

But she scooted forward and started feeling through the grass as well. We both sent furtive glances at the flying thing. It continued to be silhouetted against the bright sky, a dark shadow.

"It's coming!"

I looked up. This time, we were already on the ground, it would get us for sure. I swept my hands through the grass in desperation.

"Got it!" I yelled and thrust my hand into the grass. I yanked up the ball, grass and all.

"Go!" she yelled.

I looked at the skies. I had maybe two seconds before whatever the huge flying creature was swooped down and grabbed me. I took a deep breath, grasped the magic ball harder, gathered my shield, and thought of the room we'd just left. I lurched forward. There was a bright flash, and I opened my eyes. I was back in Dana's training room. I felt a sense of elation until I looked down. I was standing inside her big wooden table where she created her magic balls.

I almost screamed, but instead I froze. Luckily Dana was only a fraction of a second behind me, and she reappeared in the open spot we'd abandoned when we first *walked* out. I was panting with terror, while she smirked at me.

"You are an accomplished realm walker, I see." Her snark was warranted. I had been a little haughty about my skills earlier.

"What do I do?" My voice came out in a squeak.

"Did you drop the ball, again?" she asked.

I would have laughed at the saying if I wasn't sure I was going to die embedded in a table.

I opened my hand. The ball was there in a wad of grass.

"The ball is your protection. You can simply walk out of the table. You aren't injured." She crossed her arms and waited.

I clasped the ball hard and closed my eyes. I took a step forward, two steps. I was holding my breath, afraid to do more than move slowly through the table. I could feel the odd nauseating sensation of having a table slide through my guts and then disappear. I opened my eyes, and looked around, astonished. My hands grasped my abdomen. I was out and unharmed as she'd promised.

I sagged with relief, almost falling to my knees.

"That is why you need to practice with a teacher. You won't always be lucky like you were that first time."

"I didn't mean to, the first time."

"Hmmm, now, make a light ball, let's check your magic."

"Why aren't you coming down off an adrenaline rush like me?" I asked her. Refusing to comply.

"I didn't realm walk into a table."

"I'm talking about the hunter thing. You were just as terrified as I was."

She smirked, and I wanted to rip her horsey face off.

Realization hit me like a Mack truck. "That was fake!" I yelled at her.

She guffawed, sounding for all the world like a braying donkey.

"Why?" The anger vanished and I felt hurt. Betrayed. I must like and trust Dana more than I knew, or I wouldn't feel this way.

She shrugged—nonplussed about my reaction. "It is a training exercise. If you pass it, you can face anything on a realm walk."

"Did I pass?" I asked hopefully, trying to push the hurt away.

Her deadpan stare answered me. Right. I walked back into a table. I nodded at her and prepared to do it again.

We went back and forth to the training area several times—scary flying hunter, no longer needed—until Dana felt I wouldn't make any more mistakes on that run, anyway. She dismissed me.

Poor Megan and Mr. Mittens. I was sure they thought we'd return home immediately but knowing we were so close, yet so far away, had to be equally disappointing for them, even more so, since they needed me to go home—Megan because I had to take her, and Mr. Mittens since there was no point in him going home without me.

So, when I returned from lessons, I made it a point to gather us together and spend time planning what we would do when we returned. We thought of different scenarios, and what we'd do for each. But without knowing what was happening back home, they were all nothing but supposition. Still, it was something to do.

At the end of the week, my grandfather's spymaster brought news. Megan, Mr. Mittens, and I gathered in his office to hear what he'd learned recently about Sofia. The spymaster, whose name was Elegurd, was a strange little Fae. He was grizzled and stooped. His face looked like a dried apple, and he was barely as tall as my navel.

I didn't ask because I wasn't sure if it was rude, but he had to be a gnome or a dwarf or something. He didn't seem infirm, so he had to be just an example of his kind, whatever that was. The room was large and sort of stuffy. It was overly warm and crowded with furniture, books, and papers. I looked for somewhere to sit, but I was afraid to move anything off the chairs. He sat behind a desk that dwarfed him and was even large for us, but it needed to be because it was covered with different magical paraphernalia that I couldn't identify.

We stood impatiently, shifting from foot to foot, looking around, and waiting for him to talk. It took a while for him to look up, as he was intent on something that looked like a crystal ball. He wore coke-bottle glasses, and when he finally looked up at us, his eyes looked as large as an owl's. He blinked at us a couple of times, then laughed and took off the glasses.

"Sorry, I didn't see you there."

I couldn't imagine how he didn't see us, but maybe the glasses were just for looking into crystal balls.

"The human that you are looking for has been located. She is hiding in the court of an ousted Summer Lord. This is very bad. Very bad indeed."

He must be talking about the Swamp Lord. We sort of already knew that, I thought.

Megan and I looked at each other, confused. "Why is that bad?" Megan asked.

"Oh, they are plotting, plotting!" he continued, the repetition seemed to be how he spoke.

"If the Summer Lord has been ousted, what kind of trouble can they get into?" I asked, and Megan nodded.

"He has been looking for magical support to rise against the King! Against the King!"

This must have started after their bid to marry Sofia to the king. Idiots. His repetition was growing annoying, but this was the best info we'd had so far. Proof she was deeply involved with the swamp thing as Megan liked to call him. How had she stumbled on the one person that would put up with her nonsense, even desire it? This was terrible luck.

"Are they close to doing that?" Megan asked as I thought.

"They have an army, an army!"

Shit. Would she bring that army to earth or against the king? It seemed foolish to bring an army against the king. Was she that nuts? Did her ambition have no limits?

"I must inform my lord immediately, immediately!" The little man said and scurried away.

We watched him leave.

"I've got to go to Dana, we have to go home now. If that

army is headed to Earth, we won't be able to stand against them. If they are going against the king here, there isn't anything we can do to help. I need to warn everyone."

Megan looked at me, defeat showing in her eyes. "Yeah, we do. If she is bringing an army against us, we're screwed."

I felt the same, but all I could do was try to fight. "I've got to try."

Regardless of what she did here, I knew she'd bring someone back to try and defeat us. Even one trained Fae warrior, or magic user was enough to defeat us. It was demoralizing and defeating, but I had to try. I left Megan to go back to her chambers alone and headed to Dana's lab.

"Dana, we have to go back, now," I said as I opened the door. She and my grandfather turned to face me. I didn't know he was there. They both had serious looks on their faces. I guess the spymaster, for all he looked old and infirm, had imparted the bad news.

My grandfather nodded and stood up. He straightened his clothing, gave Dana a stiff courtly bow, and left the room. I'm sure he had plenty to do as the king's Commander.

"I'm going to have to use my meager skills to take us home. Do you think I can do it?"

She looked me up and down, her usual grim expression on her alien face. "Yes, but we still haven't used the element of time."

"Time? Why is that important?" I was really confused.

"Time doesn't flow the same between here and your realm. It can be a very short time, or several years could have passed."

"Years?" I gulped and sank to the floor in defeat.

"Get up, you fool. You have time magic, you can return to any time you wish."

I looked up at her. "Really?"

She just gave a disgusted horsey snort.

"How do I use it? The time magic?"

"You have to be able to clearly recall the time you want."

"So, if I can picture where I was when I brought us here, I can return us to the same moment?"

"More or less."

I should have been worried about that statement, but all I could think of was being there in time to help Gabe and defeat the witches for good. We'd had them on the run, then bam! I'd flashed us to Faerie and this mess. At least we'd fixed the disaster here in Faerie before we left.

"How much practice do you think I need to be able to do it?" I asked.

"How would I know until we try?"

Fair enough. She had me take her to the training realm. Then I pictured a day I remembered clearly in the past and took us back to my grandfather's castle at that instant.

I did what she said and pictured the first time we'd used the transporter room. I could see it clearly, exiting after my grandfather had picked us up that first day from the throne room. We'd been dirty, ragged, tired, and bloody in patches. It was my grandfather with his weapon and armor, Megan, Mr. Mittens in his Ragdoll form, and me.

I pictured it clearly, all of us stumbling out of the room, and I stepped forward, flash.

We appeared in the hallway in time to observe us step from the transporter. Grandfather saw us and frowned, but Dana shook her head and gestured for him to be silent. She ushered me back out of sight, but our earlier selves were too tired to look around and were dragged out of the room and into the hall.

Dana had me return us to the practice realm.

Once we were there, she said, "We are in the same time as your past self. You'll need to picture the time we left to return us."

I looked at her. I couldn't remember specifics because I hadn't been paying attention. "Umm, do I picture ourselves in the room?" I asked.

"Did you see us pop in as we were leaving?" she asked sarcastically.

"No."

"Then don't use us as a reference."

"What if I get a detail wrong?"

"Then we won't end up in the right time, will we?"

I let out a frustrated breath. Dana was a good teacher, but you couldn't expect a lot of praise or "atta boys" from her.

I took a deep breath, let it out to center myself, and hoped my visualization was correct. I took a step. Flash.

We were in the lab. There were subtle differences to what I'd pictured. I'd been wrong.

"This is not the correct time," Dana announced, just as I realized it as well.

Just then, the door opened, and Dana walked through. The two Danas stared at each other. Then the new Dana looked at me and addressed herself.

"You are in the wrong time."

The old Dana gave a curt nod and grabbed my arm. She had me open my mind to her for the correct image. Then we walked one step, and we were briefly in the practice field. And then another step and we were back in the lab, but I knew that now, we were in the right time. I breathed a sigh of relief. I think part of me wondered how I'd make it back to the correct Mr. Mittens and Megan.

"Did you learn the importance of making a mental picture?" she asked.

I nodded. Dana's lab was easy to overlook. It wasn't my space, it was often cluttered with various equipment and items, and without studying it and fixing it in my mind, I'd never get back here at a specific time. I'd do better the next time we practiced.

"Do not practice without me or Xrsrphn with you. You could be lost in time, and we'd never know where or when to find you."

That sent a chill down my spine. If I realm walked, I had to be sure. It would also be a good idea to take a seasoned companion. The idea of doing this on my own was terrifying.

I stuttered out an "OK" and fled the room. Dana was going to meet with my grandfather to help him plan for the coming war or offensive thing.

Mr. Mittens must have picked up on my disquiet because he met me a few steps outside of the lab.

"I blew it," I said to him.

He brushed up against my legs, and I bent to pet him.

What is the matter? he asked.

"I'm practicing my realm walking, but knowing where I am in time is another matter. I don't know if I'm going to be able to get us back in time to save Gabe and stop Sofia."

He purred. *I will help you.*

"Do your people use time when you realm walk as well?"

It is common.

He hadn't really answered the question, which could

mean that *he* couldn't. However, he seemed so sure, and I trusted he'd keep me safe.

I brushed my hand down his fur and up his tail before I followed him back to my room.

We will go back soon, he added.

I was losing hope, but it was time to go back, passed time, so I just nodded and smiled down at him.

Chapter Seventeen

I had one more lesson with Dana. One more before I took us all back. She was about to be too busy to deal with me, so I had to be ready to be on my own. She took me to the past on the practice world again and wanted me to return us to the right time in her lab. I knew it was coming, so I scanned the room to memorize specifics. The other part was to know how to avoid obstacles.

So far, I'd used her safety ball, but I wouldn't have that when I returned the three of us to earth. Dana wasn't going to give it to me, it stayed with the training facilities, and she didn't have one for each of us.

I was sure Mr. Mittens would be fine, but I was terrified of hurting my best friend. Unfortunately, the only way to avoid obstacles was a knowledge of your landing zone. There was also a split second—the moment before you stepped from one place to another—where an adept realm walker could sense anything near them and adjust their trajectory. My grandfather had taken that skill to another level and had used a concussive blast the first time I'd called him. I realized that was a safety response to the fact he didn't know who had summoned him. It could also be used to clear the area to avoid embedding yourself into a solid unforgiving surface. Its use was limited though. If it was something dense or heavy, the blast wouldn't move it out of the way.

Plus, I didn't know how to make a concussive blast. I didn't even know what piece of my elemental magic could do it. With my luck it was air, which was still lost.

Since I wasn't an adept realm walker, I had to be precise, choose an empty space like the parking area behind my house or the space around the altar. I did remember the night I'd *walked* us here. In fact, I couldn't get it out of my mind. I was pretty sure I could take us back close to when we'd left. I wasn't supremely confident, but that was more nervousness and anxiety than anything.

I held the purplish colored ball in my hand, set my shield, and pictured the lab the moment we left. Dana kept her cold eyes on me, narrowed, judging. The butterflies of anticipation built in my stomach, and with her hand on my shoulder, I took a step. Flash.

I must have had my eyes closed, because I opened them in the lab. It looked like what I'd pictured, and it felt right. I looked at Dana for confirmation. She gave a terse nod. I almost did a little dance but held it back in front of Dana. She'd definitely judge me. In my head, I did a fist pump. Yay, I was a verified realm walker. It terrified me, but for the first time, I was confident I'd get us home.

Now, if I could find out what Sofia's plans were, we'd be ahead of the game for once. It would be nice to finally be prepared, be a step ahead.

I might have skipped back to Megan and Mr. Mittens.

They looked at me expectantly as I bopped into Megan's room where they waited.

"Why are you so happy?" Megan asked. She was sitting in the one comfortable chair in the room, Mr. Mittens was sprawled on her bed. But his ears perked up when I walked in.

I couldn't keep the grin off my face. "I did it!"

They both gave me bored looks.

"Did what?" Megan yawned.

"I realm walked."

"Haven't you been doing that for days?" she said.

"Yeah, but this time, I did it through time. I can return us to the moment we left." This time I did a little dance and a fist pump.

Megan jumped out of the chair and did her own little dance. "Yes!"

Mr. Mittens stretched and jumped down. *When do you wish to leave?*

I looked at Megan. "What do you think? Tomorrow?"

She gave another twirl and a few more dance moves. "Yes! This vacation blows. I give Faerie two stars."

"It hasn't gone down from the last time?" I laughed.

She shrugged.

"Well, for me, the food brought it up, lodgings weren't bad, but everything trying to kill you? Half a star. Too bad. I don't think they're too worried about their Yelp scores," I said.

"They should be. My review will be *scathing*." Megan emphasized that with a sweeping hand gesture.

I laughed. "I'm sure they will be devastated and will change their entire society."

"And that's the power I wield in these." She spread her fingers and waved them in classic jazz fingers. She danced a minute more, then went to the wardrobe and threw it open. "I'm taking a couple of these home as well. I've never had anything so soft and silky."

"Well, get a different color from me, I'm taking the blue."

"Fine. Whatevs."

We laughed some more and flopped on her bed like teenagers at a sleepover. "I know I said I loved the food, but the thing I'm looking forward to most is an old-fashioned, greasy, cheesy pizza covered in all the meats," she said.

I looked over at her. "That sounds divine."

"Then, I want to take a shower. Not a bath, a long, hot shower with all the good smelly stuff. Then I want to go to the movies."

"No more magical bug vision?"

"Hell, no!"

I laughed at her. "Me either, I loved spending time with my grandfather, but I don't ever want to come back here. No matter how much magic there is, or how good the air makes me feel."

She held out her fist for me to bump. "Sista."

We laid on the bed for several minutes more until I started to drift off. I shook it off and gave Megan a nudge. "Let's go down and eat with my grandfather and say our goodbyes." We both struggled up. Mr. Mittens was already waiting, his kitty stomach ready.

We were almost to the door when the servant brought the summons to dinner. "Perfect timing," I mumbled.

"Let's hope your timing is this good tomorrow," Megan added.

I nodded and even Mr. Mittens gave a soft, *Hmph,* in agreement.

Before we left, we had to check on Sofia. Elegurd the spymaster was back at his desk, his glasses on and a crystal ball in front of him.

"Yes, yes I have news, news," he said after I asked about Sofia. Megan looked at me, having noticed the repetitions seemed worse today.

"What the hell?" she mouthed to me.

I shrugged. I didn't know.

We waited for him to remove his glasses and focus on us.

"The witch is planning to bring the army against the king in support of her Summer Lord. This is disturbing, very disturbing."

"Have you found out if she has plans to return to Earth?" I asked.

His focus seemed to be all over the place, which to be honest, seemed to be the opposite of what you wanted in a spymaster, but he probably had other skills that I didn't know about.

"Yes, yes." He nodded fiercely and searched his desk. He found something and pulled it out. He read it over and handed it to me. "This, this is what you need to know!"

I thanked him, and having been clearly dismissed, the three of us left to gather in my room.

Once the door shut behind us, Megan said, "Well, don't keep us waiting, what does it say?"

I looked at the paper. It was covered with pictures, and tiny words were randomly placed over the page, but as I stared at it, everything seemed to slip into a pattern. I realized it was spelled. If I hadn't been who I was, the page would have continued to look like someone had doodled all over their notes. Finally, it settled, and I could see the content clearly.

"Look at this," I said to Megan, who leaned over to see what I was indicating.

"What is it?" she asked.

"You don't see the diagram?"

She shook her head. "It looks like some middle school kid's notes."

I chuckled. "This is so cool. Only I can see the correct information. This rocks."

"So, what does it say about Sofia?" She redirected me.

"Yeah, sorry. Umm, according to the diagram, she is two villages over from the High King's palace." I squinted at some tiny script. "She is still with the same Summer Lord whose unfortunate title is 'The Lord of Swamps.'"

"I'm sure he's a pleasant sort," she remarked with a half-smile.

I moved my finger along to some more interesting information. "Here, Sofia is mentioned. Apparently, she has her magic back, and being in Faerie, she's apparently super charged. Joy."

"Just what we need." Megan sighed.

"We could bail, our fight is back home," I added.

"Yeah, but she's our problem. We can't leave that for your grandfather." Megan was being the voice of reason. I was still hoping someone here would kill Sofia. She'd involved herself in local politics after all.

The wind was seriously going out of my sails with this one. "Yeah." I sighed. "She's Earth's problem and our problem. The Fae can deal with the swamp lord. We have to take her back with us, or she'll end up in charge and ruin any future dealings with Faerie. Damn. At least on Earth, she only has one piece of Fae magic, here she's drowning in it."

"Are you suggesting what I think you're suggesting?" Megan asked.

"Do you disagree?"

"No, but I was hoping something would eat her."

I was not. If anything is going to eat her, it will be me, Mr. Mittens weighed in.

Right. He'd promised. She'd probably give him heartburn, though.

"She's yours, Mr. Mittens," I reassured him.

"OK. We go home, make our plans, come back at this moment, and take her back to Earth. Then, it's up to Mr. Mittens." I grinned down at him.

As you wish, pet.

Chapter Eighteen

We *walked* back to earth just in time to see ourselves disappear from the clearing in the left-over flash. It was still the night we'd battled the witches. We hadn't seen ourselves arriving at the time, being too involved in the fight. I wanted to cheer and give a little fist bump to Megan upon our safe arrival, but we were still in the middle of a witch war. Sofia was gone, having just been whisked to Faerie with us. Thinking about the time differences made my head hurt, so instead, I rushed back to the altar to check on Gabe.

The werewolves, Goch, and Brightfeather had routed the witches during my magic battle with Sofia, and several witches lay dead in the clearing. We could see the mounds of black clad bodies in the light of the bonfire and the moon. The Whelans were gathered around the few that were left standing, but the witches looked completely defeated. The giant wolves had them cowering near the altar. The wolves looked at us strangely, since Megan and I wore Faerie robes rather than the jeans, t-shirts, and jackets we'd been in moments ago.

Gabe was still lying on the ground where he'd been dumped for what seemed like forever ago. I rushed over to him. He was still unconscious but breathing. Megan helped me pull him up and prop him against the altar. He stirred. I hoped that was a good sign he'd wake up soon.

A wolf peeled off from the group and shifted, pulling a black robe from a dead witch and wrapping it around him.

"What is going on?" Luke asked, staring at us or Megan, anyway.

She skipped over and threw her arms around his neck. He hugged her back with one arm, the other occupied holding on to the robe.

"We've been in Faerie!" she announced with a little flourish of her arms.

Luke choked and covered it with a cough. "What?"

"Faerie, you know." She put her fingers next to her head to pantomime pointed ears.

It looked more like devil horns, but I wasn't going to ruin her fun.

"You were just here a few seconds ago," Luke said, in an attempt to understand.

"Yeah, but we were in Faerie for months, luckily Brigid figured out her magic, and poofed us back here at the same time we left!"

He blinked a couple of times, the wheels in his head catching up with her announcements. "OK. That explains the clothes."

Megan looked down at herself. "Yes! You have to lurve this fabric, here, feel." She twisted and jutted out a hip for Luke to pet her.

He smiled and swept a hand slowly from her shoulder, down her side to her waist, and over her backside. She waggled her eyebrows at him. He pulled her in and kissed her.

I waited a moment or two. When the other wolves began rolling their eyes, I cleared my throat. "Um, hate to interrupt, but we have witches."

Luke and Megan pulled apart reluctantly. He mumbled, "Witches." Then his eyes sharpened. "Witches, where's Sofia? You two and the cat ran after her."

"Yup," Megan said. "Plot twist. She's in Faerie."

The tension in Luke's shoulders relaxed, and they dropped an inch.

I hated to ruin Megan's fun, but I had to. "Let's take this group to the house, we have to talk." I cast a light ball and raised it up to illuminate our trek back.

There were only five witches that remained alive or were caught before they'd fled. Luke and Noah, who were both on two legs and now clad in witch robes, picked Gabe up under the armpits, slung his arms around their necks, and began the long walk back. The remaining Whelans in wolf form nipped at the heels of the captured witches until they started to move. After greeting us, Goch and Bright-feather flew back to the house to meet our captives, Megan and I trailing behind. Mr. Mittens brought up the rear to watch for any of the escaped witches who might try to take advantage of the situation. We were a motley crew.

We broke through the woods, finally. The little Fae slippers Megan and I wore were barely better than being barefoot, and we stumbled and complained the whole way back. My house never looked so good. I wanted to run up and give it a hug, but I held myself back. I'd look like an idiot if I did that. Mr. Mittens did run ahead and jump up on the railing of the back porch. He loved to sit there; it gave him a vantage point.

Since everyone was faster than us, the witches were in a group in the yard, Goch and Brightfeather keeping their eyes on them. I lifted my light ball into the air until it lit up the back area like a streetlight. The Whelans had shifted back and dressed. Luke and Noah had deposited Gabe in the house on his bed upstairs to recover from the spell and had dressed in their regular clothes as well. I considered going in and putting on jeans and a sweater. But there wasn't any point in any more delay.

I had to decide what to do with the witches, so I had Mr. Mittens, Megan, and the Whelans gather in the kitchen to decide what to do with the ones that were left.

"Kill them," Noah said, coldly. The Whelans were still rightly upset about their father's death.

Mr. Mittens's vote was the same, not that I expected anything different from him. He had a strict "kill first, ask questions later" belief system.

"We should find out all they know before we do anything," Megan added.

Everyone agreed that was a definite point.

"I just want to bring up this point and discuss the pros and cons, so don't get upset." I took a deep breath. "What would happen if we just let them go?"

I expected some arguing from the wolves, but they took a moment to consider before they answered.

"Cons," Noah started. "They gather up their evil buddies and come back, or they involve other supernatural races and start a war against us."

"Pros," Madison added, "They all move out of town and no more witches will bother us."

"Not likely," Noah snorted.

"Look, they are beaten, if we kill them at this point,

then we are the murderers. I say let them go. We can make them swear an oath or something," Izzy said.

"Will they keep it if we do?" Megan asked, hopefully.

"If it's on their magic, they won't have a choice," Izzy added.

"That's a thing?" I asked because if it was, that was the best solution in my book.

Izzy shrugged. "I've heard about it. Anyone else know for sure?" She looked around at her family.

Anna, who had remained quiet, finally chimed in. "Yes, and that is the best solution."

Noah started to protest, but a flash of her green eyes shut him up. He might be the new alpha, but his mama was still in charge of the family.

"Agreed?" she asked.

The vote wasn't unanimous, Mr. Mittens still thought we should kill them all.

We walked out and faced the witches who were sobbing and clinging to each other. It could have been the dragon looming over them, but they didn't know he was a sweet kid at heart.

I can eat them, Lady Brigid. I'd be happy to! Goch said, and I knew that everyone heard when the witches reacted by cowering further.

"Thanks, Goch, we decided to let them go."

He looked dejected at that, and I felt bad. "You did such a great job, you are welcome to eat any witches we left behind in the clearing."

He brightened. *Thank you so much!* he said and launched himself in the air, his wing beats blasting us and sending dust and leaves swirling around. At least I wouldn't have to sink those bodies into the ground. Plus, it added a layer of intimidation for the living ones.

I stood before the five witches. "We've come to an understanding." I looked at my companions and they all nodded. "We will release you to your lives if you are willing to take a magical oath."

A few witches stood a little taller, hope shining on their faces. A brave woman stepped forward. "What oath?"

"It's a simple thing. You swear on your magic to never come against us again in any way."

The speaker frowned, but she turned to the others, and they spoke quietly to each other. I guess she had made herself the speaker because she turned back. "If we don't?"

Death, Mr. Mittens answered for me, morphing into his Splintercat form before them and snarling.

They cringed back, but the spokeswitch just closed her eyes briefly, tension in her form.

I nodded. I didn't need to say anything more.

"We accept. Under one condition."

I looked at my companions and mouthed, "condition?" I turned back to the witches. "What is it?"

They looked at each other. "You protect us from Sofia. She will kill us if we don't obey her."

That seemed fair, and I didn't doubt for a minute that once she learned of their perceived betrayal, she would kill them.

"Agreed. We have plans for her, anyway."

She's mine, my cat broadcast, with an image of him leaping on her and crushing her to the ground.

The witches each took the oath, and we allowed them to leave. They wandered back in the direction of the altar. I wanted to remind them there was a dragon feasting back there, but I let it go. They'd figure it out.

I thanked Brightfeather, and she flew off. That left the wolves, me, Megan, and Mr. Mittens. We gathered in my kitchen to hear about our adventures on another world and my plans to defeat Sofia.

Chapter Nineteen

After everyone left, and Megan was taking her "glorious" hot shower, I went up to Gabe's room to check on him. He was still asleep. But when I shook him, he stirred, and his eyes opened briefly. It seemed that whatever spell had been laid on him was wearing off. I figured I'd give him another hour before I really got worried and attempted to remove the spell. I didn't know if the spell I had used on him before would work for this, but I'd try if he hadn't awakened by then.

Megan was in the kitchen dressed in flannel PJ bottoms and a soft cotton top. She had her phone and was scrolling through it.

"I'm ordering pizza. What do you want?" she said.

"The usual, but get double, Gabe will be starving when he wakes up, I'm sure."

"Got it." She called the number and placed the order for delivery.

"Thanks, I'm gonna take a shower."

I went into my marvelous bathroom, took a shower of

my own, and changed into my own clothes. No matter how lovely the fabrics we'd worn in Faerie were, they just couldn't beat my broken-in jeans and long-sleeved t-shirt for comfort.

After, I wandered back to the kitchen, filled a glass of water, and drank it down. For whatever reason, realm walking was thirsty work. "I'm gonna go check on Gabe," I said to Megan.

She waved me away, still scrolling through her phone.

"I thought you'd be hanging out with Luke?" I said as I passed her.

"I told him tomorrow, I'm tired, and so was he." I bet she was. I was exhausted with the feeling of *extra* jet lag. The last time I'd realm walked extra people with me, I'd been too exhausted from the marching to notice the extra fatigue. Since I'd already been tired from practicing almost non-stop with Dana, dragging a non-magical person with me was even more fatiguing.

I dragged myself up the stairs to the second floor, anxiety increasing with every step. I knocked on Gabe's door softly, but he didn't respond. My heart fell. I was so sure he'd be awake by now. I opened the door and walked in. He wasn't on the bed, but the shower was running. I smiled.

I debated waiting, but I wanted him to know I was here, so I knocked on the partially closed bathroom door.

"Gabe?"

"I'll be out in a second," he answered.

"OK, I'll wait by the bed." I walked over and sat on his bed.

Soon enough, I heard the water shut off and the sound of the glass door opening and shutting. A minute later, he came out, damp hair tousled, a towel wrapped around his hips. My mouth fell open. He was beautiful. All firm flesh and defined muscles. Did he work out? Or was this just the way he was made?

He chuckled, a deep rumbling sound that I felt in my bones.

I closed my mouth. "Are you feeling alright?" I asked, my voice squeaky. I cleared my throat and tried to get a hold of myself.

"Yes, why?" he asked. Was it possible he was unaware of Sofia's latest ploy? Surely, he remembered being kidnapped at the clinic. I did, and it had been months for me.

"Because you were kidnapped and held captive by the witch bitch Sofia," I stated.

He frowned. "That really happened? It seems like a bad dream. How long ago?"

I had to think back. How long had she had him after she'd captured him at the clinic?

"Just the day, I think?"

He looked confused.

"Sorry, I forgot you were asleep when we told the others about our little adventure. We've been in Faerie for almost two months. I realm walked us back to the moment when I accidentally realm walked."

"Us?" he asked confused.

"Oh, yeah, umm, me, Megan, Mr. Mittens, and Sofia…" I trailed off.

He sat on the bed and pulled me into a hug. His shower hot skin blazed against me. I laid my head on his chest and smelled the scent of his soap and beneath it, him.

"That's wild. You'll have to fill me in on what happened there. What was it like?"

"Um, mostly terrifying." My hand was unconsciously

exploring the firm muscles of his back. And my mind was not on the conversation. His voice grew huskier.

"I'm sorry, Bridge."

I kissed his neck and mumbled into his skin, "It's OK."

He groaned and reached down to tilt my head up to meet his lips.

I buried my hands in his hair and kissed him back. He tasted like toothpaste. I smiled against his lips, before I was sucked back under by the heat of his kiss, the warmth of his tongue, and the hardness of his body. He eased me down on the bed, and I pulled him to me, my heart beating hard and fast. His weight pressed me into the mattress, and I moaned into his mouth.

Before things went too far, the doorbell rang. I almost ignored it, since Megan was downstairs, but it was probably the pizza, and she'd just come up here looking for us. I kissed him one last time.

"We gotta go. That's the pizza," I said with a smile.

His eyes were dark and half lidded. He rolled off me onto his back, his towel barely covering him. "I'm gonna need a minute," he said. "I'll see you down there."

I grinned. Looking at his towel, I could see he would need a minute. "OK, see you in a minute. I leaned down and kissed him again.

"Stop doing that, or I'll be up here a lot longer," he remarked.

I dragged myself away and shut his door behind me.

I smiled all the way down the stairs. I'd missed him so much. And he was here, he remembered me, and he wanted me as much as I wanted him. Life, for the moment, was good.

When I entered the kitchen, Megan took one look at me, and said, "Spill. You couldn't have gotten too far in the few minutes you've been up there, but that is a serious loved up look."

I nodded. "We just kissed, but *what* a kiss." I sighed. "Now, he's getting dressed, so quit with the questions. I'll get the plates."

She laughed. "He's getting dressed? What did you do to him in…" She looked at her wrist like she wore a watch. "Three point five minutes?"

I scoffed. "He was just getting out of the shower. Stop."

"So, he was nakey?" She waggled her eyebrows.

I rolled my eyes. "There might have been a towel."

"Did it stay on?"

"Unfortunately."

She giggled, and then we had to shut up, because we could hear him coming down the stairs.

I set the table, and Megan tossed the salad she'd started and placed the bowl on the table.

When Gabe entered the kitchen, we were the picture of non-gossipy domesticity.

We started to eat. Megan was in her element, dipping her pizza in ranch dressing and declaring it better than Faerie food, when Mr. Mittens walked into the kitchen. At first, I assumed he was just ready for his supper, but I turned to look at him, and I saw fear in his eyes.

I jumped up, rocking the chair back slightly. "What's wrong?"

She's here.

My stomach fell. My face flushed with heat. I didn't need to ask, but I did. "Who is here?"

Sofia. She's brought an army.

Shit.

Megan and Gabe leapt up. Megan grabbed her phone,

and so did Gabe, they were calling the werewolves. I put out a mental call to Goch and Brightfeather.

Even with our few allies, how could we stand against an army?

"What do we do?" I asked, but it was mainly to myself. My mind raced. What options did we have?

We are already fighting, Goch's mental voice was faint, and I was worried about my two charges, creatures who came to *me* for safety. If Sofia brought an army, that meant she had more than one magic user with her. How could she transport more than a few people at a time from Faerie? How had she known when and where to bring them? This couldn't be!

My mind flicked to a conversation about the transporter rooms. You only needed a clear picture to any place to use them. I was sure Sofia's memory of my clearing and the altar was as clear in her mind as it was in mine. My fists clenched.

"How many?" I asked my cat.

They were still arriving when I walked here, he said. *Dozens?*

Dozens. That meant they weren't quite ready, more were probably still arriving. I had time. Time. I had time magic! I could do something. I hoped I could beat her.

"I have an idea. Please trust me. Stay away from her, stay safe. I'll be right back."

I took a step, and there was a bright flash.

Chapter Twenty

I stepped into my grandfather's study. He looked up at me in surprise.

"Didn't you just leave?" he asked.

My Earth clothes were a big hint that I had indeed.

"Yes. I need your help," I said.

He must have heard the desperation because his eyes sharpened, and he became more alert. "What's the matter?"

"Sofia, my witch nemesis…" I took a deep breath and tried to slow my heart rate. I was sweating and breathing like I'd run a race. "She's brought an army from Faerie to my house. I need help, there are so few of us, and I'm the only magic user. She faked us out, Grandfather. She decided to hit us first, not the king. Can you help me?"

He stood. "Yes, I owe you a favor, if this is how you wish it repaid, I'm honored."

I'd forgotten about the thanks I'd given him. I felt a tug in my chest, demanding a response. "Yes, this will follow your obligation."

There was a snap, and a wave of rightness zinged through me.

Grandfather gave me a Fae nod, "How many did she have with her?"

"Mr. Mittens said dozens."

"I believe we can borrow some of the king's Scáthanna. He owes us. But the only magic users will be you, myself, and Dana."

"I don't know how many magic users she has with her, but that'll have to do."

He tilted his head and folded his arms over his massive chest. "It might only be herself, the swamp lord and one other from what my spymaster has been telling me."

I nodded. This could work. The panic was starting to die down. The pizza I'd eaten had decided maybe it would stay in my stomach.

"Do you have thirteen elements, too, Grandfather?" I asked him. I hadn't dared before.

He looked at me strangely. "Yes, how else do you think it came to you?" he asked, simply.

"OK." I took another deep breath. "What about Dana?" I remembered the court gossip, and how the king only had seven. Could Dana have more? Was she also his equal? Had my grandfather been keeping more than one secret from the king?

He smiled. "Don't worry about Dana. She's got a few tricks up her sleeves."

Right, not his secret to share. I wondered if being half-Kelpie gave her gifts the rest of the Fae didn't have. I'd have to watch her in the fight if I could.

He closed his eyes, and I realized he was sending out telepathic messages. That was handy. Maybe someday, I'd be a strong enough telepath I could do that. I could usually contact people on my land, but I hadn't tried anyone off my land. I guess my magic was strongest there and here.

"Grandfather, I've got to go back, can I give you the mental picture you need to arrive at the right place and time?"

He gave me the Fae head bob, and I reconstructed the exact place and time in my mind and pushed it to him.

"She's gonna arrive about an hour from the time I just gave you. It should give you a little time to prepare an ambush. Just remember, wait until the griffin and the dragon have engaged, otherwise we'll screw up the timeline I'm building. OK?"

"Yes, child. I've been in a few battles and realm walked a couple of times in my day."

I laughed nervously. "Yeah. I'm counting on that. Hope your swamp lord is an idiot."

"Appears to be. He's picked a fight with the wrong Fae family, hasn't he?"

"Hope so." I gave him a wan smile, fixed my destination and my shield in place, and *walked* back in a flash of light.

I stepped back into my kitchen, pizza boxes strewn about, my friends standing where I'd left them less than a second ago.

"That was fast," Gabe said.

I smiled at him and waggled my fingers. "Time magic."

He pulled me into him, and I wrapped my arms around him.

Megan reached forward and grabbed my arm. "What did he say?"

"If all went well, he's been here for an hour preparing a trap. Gabe, Mr. Mittens and I are heading out. You should stay, lock yourself in the attic. I think I left it open forever ago."

She scoffed. "Hell, no." She pulled two of Dana's magic balls from her pocket. "While you were getting pampered at queen class, and then languishing in prison, Mr. Mittens has been helping your grandfather's master at arms train me to be a badass." She activated one of the balls, and a seven-foot-long spear appeared in her hands.

"No way you could keep that from me," I said, incredulously. I pulled away from Gabe and put my hands on my hips. I stared at my cat, pointing an accusatory finger at him. "You either."

"There were hints; you just didn't pick up on it. I was gonna surprise you." She paused, held out her arm without the spear, waved a jazz hand, and said, "Surprise…"

I sighed and looked at my cat.

I'm a cat. If I wish to keep a secret, no one will ever know it, Mr. Mittens remarked smugly.

I rolled my eyes. "How much of a badass are you?" I asked Megan.

"Well, I had almost two months of training, so…I know where the pointy end goes," she said with a shrug. "I also have this." She whispered something and activated the other ball, and a shield appeared in her hand. "This one is handy because it protects me all the way around. Magical shield, baby!"

I squinted at her. "What were your activation words?"

"Why? You gonna take my magic balls away?" she asked with an edge of suspicion.

"No, because I swear you just said, 'It's just a flesh wound?'" I said.

She smirked. "You got it in one."

I rolled my eyes. "What was the one for the shield? Still from the Holy Grail?"

"Maybe…" She looked away.

I sighed again and waved my hand, letting her keep her secrets. I wasn't keeping her out of the fight. Frankly, she now had a lot more fighting experience than I did, and I'd never be able to convince her to hang back.

"Gabe, do you have a weapon?" I asked.

He looked at me funny. "No, I am a weapon."

I remembered he'd told me the other side to being a magical healer, but I didn't know how it worked. He could give life force and fill a well of power, but he could take it away as well. I hoped he didn't have to touch anyone to do that, or he would be vulnerable.

I was scared—terrified even—that I would be sending my friends to their deaths, but I couldn't stop them. How did my life end up like this? Why did I drag those I loved the most into this mess? I twisted my focus ring on my finger —a nervous habit I'd developed when I was married to Evan. I dropped my hands. This wasn't the same. Unlike Evan's bullshit, this was real and had hard and lasting consequences to others besides me. I took a deep breath and centered myself. Game face.

"Fine. I'm gonna wrap us all in shadow for camouflage, and we're heading to the field where Mr. Mittens said they were fighting. Meg, it's the field by the dairy. Remember how to get there in case we get separated?"

"Yup."

I'll transform outside, then wrap me in shadow, Mr. Mittens said.

"Ok, here we go." We walked out so Mr. Mittens could shift. Once he was in his Splintercat form, I reached my hand out for Gabe, since he wouldn't see me once we were camouflaged. Megan, whose hands were full, was partnering with Mr. Mittens. He would stay close so he could touch and guide her. He always knew where *I* was. Gabe grasped my hand. I wrapped the four of us in shadow, and we headed out to stop the evil witch.

I was a little premature with the camouflage because I had to renew it right before we arrived at the field. But in my defense, I was super nervous and terrified.

Gabe kept tight hold of my hand, and Mr. Mittens made sure he rubbed against me. He always seemed to forget his size while in Splintercat form, and I rocked against Gabe's side. He steadied me, physically, so I didn't fall over, and emotionally as his presence centered me. We were finally together. I wouldn't let a witch or something else separate us again.

The field had been brush-hogged. So, the grass was short, and the weeds and blackberry bushes were gone. In the spring, I'd have it tilled, fertilized, and planted with a hay mix of grasses for my herbivore clients—if we survived. And for those that weren't, the grass would feed the stock I'd use for their eating pleasure. There were several fields that the fences had recently been removed from, and that's where Sofia had placed her army to prepare them for the attack on my house. I hoped she was surprised we found her out before she reached it.

Goch and Brightfeather were busy harassing the troops. Goch's fire was keeping them held down, which was good, and I hoped he wasn't getting injured from the spears and arrows being shot at him. Brightfeather was cannier about her attacks, and being naturally camouflaged under the color of the usually grey sky helped her avoid being wounded. I so wanted to send them off to keep them from getting hurt. But I knew they wouldn't stop. They took their gratitude to me and their friendship to the limits. My heart swelled with love for them, and my eyes filled with tears. The best thing I could do was send in help to relieve them.

I sent the pre-arranged signal to my grandfather telepathically, hoping he was really here and ready with his ambush. There was one terrifying second while I waited for a reply. If he wasn't here, we were screwed and everyone I loved would die. My heart fluttered in my chest, and I held my breath.

It didn't come in my mind as I expected, but suddenly, I heard the pounding of hooves, and from the copse of trees to our left, a group of about twenty *Baincapall* warriors burst out and gallop toward Sofia and her army.

I wanted to cheer, but that would defeat the purpose of being cloaked. Grandfather, Dana, Gabe, and I were the magical backup. We needed to keep that element of surprise.

A shout went up from Sofia's army, and I saw her swamp lord barking out orders. I knew it was him because he shot a magical blast of fire at my dragon. Foolish, dragons were most definitely fireproof. Goch responded with a massive blast of dragon fire, and swamp lord ducked down and cowered. Sofia threw up a shield of ice. It melted in the wake of the dragon fire, and I wanted to laugh.

That's the moment they noticed the king's Scáthanna, their troops turning and rushing to meet them. I sent a mental call to Goch and Brightfeather to move to the opposite side and try to drive the enemy towards the first wave of our attackers.

We were close enough now that a stray magical attack almost hit us, and I figured it was time to do our part.

"Ready, Gabe?" I whispered.

"Ready."

"Mr. Mittens and Megan are you ready?"

"Yup."

Yes.

I sent my grandfather a telepathic, "*We're in position.*"

This was better than walkie talkies.

When I give the signal, hit them with lightning, was the reply.

"Ok, Gabe," I whispered. "We're about to be up."

He squeezed my hand in acknowledgement.

The signal came, and using my left hand, I sent a lightning bolt into the mass of the enemy. Our shadow camouflage fell, and we were in the battle.

Mr. Mittens charged in and started annihilating Fae warriors. His claws and teeth were a blur, and soon he was surrounded in a mist of red as heads rolled and bodies stacked up around him. He reminded me a little of the Tasmanian Devil in the Bugs Bunny cartoons—only the R-rated version. A whirling dervish of death.

Megan made herself our protector as we used our magic to fight. I engaged a soldier close to me. I smacked him with a blast a fire, and he fell, screaming to the ground, roasting in his silvery armor. Megan skewered another I hadn't seen to my left.

Gabe had to be close—at least two feet—it appeared, but once he was near, soldiers left and right dropped courtesy of his death gift. It took a few seconds for each non-magical soldier to succumb. Probably because his gift worked by draining the well of life force. Since he was the most vulnerable, Megan and I stayed close and tried to keep him protected. I watched as Megan blocked with her shield or cut soldiers down with her spear. She *was* a badass.

Soon, I couldn't tell what was happening or who was winning the day. It was a mess of troops, *Baincapall*, magic, and magical creatures. I threw out fire and lightning at anyone I didn't recognize and tried to keep Gabe protected on one side, while Megan took the other. Luckily, he could heal himself and Megan if the wounds weren't grievous, and they both picked up many of those.

I caught a glimpse of my grandfather once, being taller than most and savage. He hacked with his ax and threw magic with his off hand. It was amazing to see him in action. I had no doubt why he was the king's Pendragon. I hadn't seen Dana yet, but my attention had to remain focused.

I don't know how long the battle went on, but eventually, I caught a glimpse of Sofia. In the murky darkness, lit only by magic and torches, she looked harder than she had before Faerie and fiercer. Her hair was braided back, and she was dressed in armor and held a spear not unlike Megan's. Our eyes met.

She saw me. She pointed the spear at me and screamed, "You!" She ran towards me. Or tried to. We both fought through the crowds to meet. I threw spells right and left. I caught Sofia from the corner of my eye flinging her spear at a *Baincapall*; the warrior snatched it from the air and used it against another foe. Sofia screamed her rage.

Her real spear gone; Sofia formed an ice spear as she drew within throwing range of me. I reached into the earth and drew up a barrier just as she flung it. The earth caught it, and I yanked it down deep under the ground. She screeched and launched her ice darts at me. I met them with fire. She was stronger. Much stronger. Faerie had been good to her magic. But she forgot one thing, it had also been good to mine.

My fire melted them easily, and she frowned. She formed another ice spear and jabbed it at me. I melted it away.

"How are you doing this!" she bellowed at me.

"I'm no longer the beginner you've been taking advantage of. I'm Fae." I sent the lightning at her. She jumped back and stumbled. But she pulled up an ice shield in time. I blasted it over and over until it disintegrated, and for the first time, I saw fear in her eyes. She called a name, and the swamp lord joined her.

He was a Fae lord, so he had to be strong in magic. However, I had it from the entire gossipy court of the high king's servants, that no one was stronger in magic than my grandfather and by extension, me. Since my grandfather was busy kicking the swamp lord's army into dust, I figured I could take down the bastard myself. Sofia scrambled behind him, probably to take a breather. He smiled like I was foolish to stand before him. He let his fire loose.

It was a lot. The fire streamed at me, the heat flushing my skin and singing my hair. I gasped, the air almost too hot to breathe. I had fire, too. Fire, water, earth, and lightning, and I'd trained myself to hold two ready in my mind. I blocked his fire with earth and slammed a lightning bolt at him.

It crackled and flashed as it struck him. He flew back ten feet and skidded on the churned ground. Now, he looked the part of swamp lord—mud covered and slimy. His armor must have protected him from the bolt because he sprang up quickly. Sofia and Swampy fired attack after attack at me. Gabe had disappeared from my side, and I couldn't stop long enough to check on him. I hoped he was alright.

I did catch Megan out of the corner of my eye. If we'd had armor for her to wear, she'd have looked as fierce as a Valkyrie. She lunged, thrust, and blocked with her spear. When she needed to, she manifested her shield and blocked. She was truly a badass. Her weeks of training coupled with years of rage from working for Evan was doing her well.

She screamed at another opponent, and I almost turned to see if she was hurt, when I heard her yell, "I fart in your general direction."

I turned to block another ice spear and saw Megan smack down a sword attack with her shield. I grinned. Monty Python to the rescue.

Fire, ice, block, attack, lightning, water, fire—exchange after magical exchange until my arms were so tired from casting that they ached, and my blows started to miss in random directions. Since there were two of them, they were still relatively fresh, and I realized I was in trouble. The returning blows were coming faster and striking closer. I backpedaled.

The next blast of fire nearly singed my eyebrows off, and I almost sobbed in fear. I could barely lift my arms to respond. That's when I saw Gabe reach out to Sofia. She stumbled, and I whirled to him.

"Watch out!" I yelled.

Gabe's face was grim, but he didn't move; he didn't stop. I wasn't going to be in time for her next blast of magic. I gritted my teeth, reached down deep and threw the strongest lightning bolt I could muster at the swamp lord. He collapsed, twitching. I gathered up all of my strength and ran at Sofia.

Her face was distorted with hate and rage. She was hideous, her black heart and soul finally showing on her usually perfectly made-up face now streaked with mud and blood.

Gabe was attempting to empty her well, but it must have been deep and filled to the brim, because he was struggling. He had to stop her before she finished him, and I didn't think he was going to make it. She raised her hands, and I could feel the air temperature drop as she reached for the ice magic. She moved them forward. I wasn't going to get there in time. I sobbed, and threw fire at her, Nothing. The magic she built shielded her. I tried lightning. It arced away. I screamed in frustration and threw myself at her.

I'd never been sporty in my youth, but I'd watched plenty of football in high school, so I knew what a tackle looked like. She launched her ice attack at Gabe just as I struck her legs, knocking them out from under her. She fell on me, and I grabbed her arm to hold her down. I couldn't see Gabe, so I didn't know if she'd hit him with her spell.

Sofia was thin. All those unhappy food choices made for one skinny bitch. I wasn't that large, but I ate, and I had all that carb energy from the pizza. Even though I wanted to vomit it up now, I rolled over her and held her arms in the mud—pinning her torso under my thighs. I could feel my own ice magic building up in her as she attempted to use it against me. But, she made one tiny mistake. It *wasn't* hers.

With the skin to skin contact of my hands on her bare arms, the power called to me, just like the pieces of jewelry. I opened myself to it, and in a flash, it left her and sank into my skin. Her face sunk slightly, giving her gaunt look, and fine lines appeared where she'd had none before. I bared my teeth at her.

She screamed in rage, "Die you Fae bitch!"

This time, she blasted me off with a witch spell. I landed on my back next to Gabe. I reached out a hand to touch him. He was cold.

"No, no, no!" I scrambled over to him and looked into his face. His eyes flicked to mine.

"I'm OK, Bridge, she stunned me, but I'm good." He struggled to sit up, and I gave a sob of relief.

He shivered. "She hit me with a glancing blow."

"Your skin is cold, I was afraid…"

We didn't have time to talk; swamp boy was back up and angry. He sent another blast of fire at us. This time, I was tired, and I did something I didn't think to do before. I had the ground swallow him. I had no idea if he had a defense against that, but I figured if he did it would give us a minute at least.

Sofia threw one more spell our way and took off running towards her army and the relative safety of her allies.

I had to end this. I had to end it now. I couldn't go through life looking over my shoulder. I couldn't let her escape to Faerie to worry my family there. She was done.

I stood, wobbly, and unsteady. Gabe reached out and steadied me. I could feel the magic all around me and in me, but I was nearing the end of my endurance. I focused all my will through my focus ring and wished Sofia back here. My cat had told me once that my inherent magic could call things to me. I just had to be careful that no one saw, and that the thing existed. Frankly, I didn't care if anyone saw. Sofia flew off her feet and sailed through the air. She splashed down at my feet.

I debated having the earth swallow her as well, but that wasn't her fate.

"Mr. Mittens!" I bellowed.

Sofia's eyes flew open wide. With her well partially drained and her Fae magic gone, she had nothing to fight with. She tried to scramble away. I heard the rumble of my cat's growl and caught him galloping towards us out of the corner of my eye. He was drenched in blood, although I couldn't see any visible wounds. He looked fierce and terrifying, and I shivered. Unlike his Ragdoll grumpy face, he almost looked happy. It was probably his huge fangs hanging below his jaw. Mud and blood were blocking his spots and usual glow, but his large body rippled with muscles as he trotted up to my side.

You rang? he said, his eyes alight with glee.

I might have let a little nervous giggle escape. My cat loved a battle.

Brigid, a mental call reached me from my grandfather.

Before I answered him, I addressed my cat. "I saved you a little something."

Sofia finally got her feet under her and started to run.

Thank you, pet. I love a good snack after a battle.

His bobbed tail twitched once, and he crouched down. Then he launched himself in a huge Splintercat flying leap. His front feet hit her in the back, and she splayed forward in the mud. I turned away just as his teeth grasped the back of her neck, and he picked her up like a doll and shook her. The crunch of her bones echoed in my mind. I shivered and felt ill.

I couldn't bear to watch my cat eat a person, even one as deserving as Sofia. I turned around and reached for Gabe's hand. *Yes, grandfather?* I replied.

"You have won the day." He strolled out of the woods on my other side, and I smiled at him. Dana and the *Baincapall* wandered through the remains of Sofia's army, those still alive were bowed in submission and being cuffed for transport back to Faerie.

My grandfather, like my cat, was covered in blood and gore. But he looked happy, refreshed even.

"I appreciate the help," I said to him.

He threw back his head and guffawed. "You saved me the trouble of mopping up this pathetic rebellion back on Faerie. I should be thanking you. I'll make sure the king knows you took care of his problem as well."

"Is everyone OK?" I asked, afraid that I'd been the cause of casualties on his side.

"An acceptable amount for a battle this size. Don't worry. It would have been worse on Faerie with the extra magic available there."

I obviously didn't have the same values, but if he wasn't angry about it, I'd let him deal with the fallout. I had to deal with the same here.

"We've already started *transporting* the prisoners back. We should be off your world in a few hours." He took a deep breath and looked around. "The magic is thicker here. It is almost bearable." He smiled at me.

"Do you have to go? You could come clean up back at the house and see what I've done to the place." He looked towards the house, although it couldn't be seen from here. "I will, soon. I promise you."

I understood, he was in charge and had his people to take care of.

"OK, I'll hold you to it," I said.

He reached out and hugged me. Both of us were filthy, but it didn't matter.

"I'm grateful for you, Grandfather."

"You are my child. I'll always be here for you," he said and then turned and walked off, barking out orders and directing his troops.

I looked for Megan and Gabe. They joined me as did Mr. Mittens. The wolves hadn't even made it to the final battle. I was sure they'd be disappointed. I smiled at my friends, and we shared muddy, bloody hugs. "It's over," I said.

It was glorious, pet, Mr. Mittens added.

Chapter Twenty-One

I stood in the grand entry and gazed up at the tree. I'd bought the largest one I could find at the lot. I guess I could have cut one down from my own property, but that would have required a whole different crew than having the people from the tree lot bring it in and set it up for me. The ceiling in this part of the house was twenty feet tall. The tree was sixteen.

I didn't know what I was thinking. How was I going to decorate this beast? I didn't own a ladder this tall. Well, I had magic. I'm sure it would make a difference when we had to put the star on top.

I had a small scar now on the top of my left arm, and I rubbed it through my shirt thoughtfully as I admired the tree. After the battle, Gabe had healed our cuts and scrapes. My grandfather had returned to Faerie with his prisoners. The wolves showed up when we were cleaning up, disappointed they hadn't been in the battle. I hadn't wanted to kill anyone, except Sofia, but after the battle ended, I realized that Swampy hadn't clawed his way out of the ground.

I'd felt bad about that for a while. I'd seriously thought he'd pop back up in a minute or two, but I guess he wasn't that strong of a magic user.

No one else felt bad about me ending him; he had tried to kill me and had planned to kill the king as well. I didn't think he needed to die for being delusional, but he did try to kill me and my friends, which was rude. We didn't even know him.

It didn't matter anymore. Sofia was gone, and the witches were handled. I turned away from the tree, the thrill of seeing it up zinged through me one more time. I smiled. Megan was practically vibrating with excitement, and even Mr. Mittens looked less grumpy. I looked down at him, sitting by my side as he gazed at the glorious noble fir.

We were going to have a party this weekend. Sort of a combination Christmas party and opening of the bed-and-breakfast. The house was finished, and everything was ready for visitors. The only scary thing was the type of guests we'd get...if we got any. We'd been working on subtly advertising to the supernatural community, and it wasn't easy.

"Did you buy enough ornaments?" Megan asked, eyeing the height and breadth of the enormously full tree.

"Umm, I'm not sure, now," I sighed. "We can do the visible parts and leave the back bare, then we'll be OK," I finished weakly.

"Yeah, that'll work. Did you finish that light spell?"

"I think so. It should work. I'll just have to renew it weekly."

She looked at me.

I looked behind me. "What?"

"Well, do it," she demanded.

I snorted. "Fine." I used my focusing ring and concentrated on creating little bits of light to cover the tree with. *Magical* twinkle lights. I figured they'd be easier than wrapping the entire behemoth in wire. I finished the creation and cast the light into the tree. It flashed brightly for a second, and all of us looked away. It subsided until the tree was afire with a multitude of tiny white lights. It was stunning.

"Whoa," Megan commented.

I nodded. It worked better than I'd hoped.

What is the purpose of the tree in the house, again? Mr. Mittens's surly mental voice interrupted my moment.

"It's traditional. A symbol of the season."

Hmpf. It is strange. There are trees outside. If you want to enjoy them, you simply can glance out the window or walk outside. He sat heavily and looked at me. His head cocked slightly as though he really were trying to figure it out. *Humans are strange.*

"I know you've seen Christmas trees before," I answered.

Hmpf. He picked up a large paw and groomed it, dismissing me. I rolled my eyes at him.

I looked back at the tree. The ornaments were supposed to be delivered tomorrow. That would give us two days to get the tree and the house decorated for the party. I sighed. I had a lot of work ahead of me. Too bad magic couldn't do everything.

I checked my phone for the time. Gabe would be here soon. My stomach fluttered, and I gave a little gasp of air. He was picking me up for a date. A real one. Now that we didn't have Sofia and her witch coven machinations hanging over us, this would feel *real*—a brand new start.

Megan threw me a knowing look. "Go do your finishing touches, I'll feed the cat."

Mr. Mittens's face grew grumpier. *Human, don't forget my*

food is in the second drawer of the refrigerator. The halibut will be adequate.

Megan glared at him. "If I don't strangle him first."

Hmpf. He strolled towards the kitchen, his floofy tail erect, a little sway to the tip of his tail and a slight glow to his fur.

I gave a flourish and bow to Megan. "Go serve your cat master with the proper deference he demands," I said in a bad English accent.

She groaned, threw her head back, raised her hands to the heavens in a fake plea of supplication, and then followed him.

"Cats," I muttered as I turned and headed to my bathroom for the final touches, as Megan had called them, to my hair and makeup and to pull on my date clothes. I was happy. My date wouldn't care that my new style consisted of jeans and long-sleeved t-shirts. That in itself was a breath of fresh air. So, I pulled on my best fitted jeans and the nicest t-shirt I owned. It was blue to bring out my eyes, and I paired it with puffy warm vest since it was cold outside.

I brushed my hair with one of those Fae brushes that smoothed the frizz. Then, I freshened up my mascara. I looked...happy. I hadn't seen this side of myself for a long time. It brightened my face, made me look younger than my forty-two years, and filled my heart with contentment.

Things were good. The Inn would open after the beginning of the year. My people were safe. My grandfather promised to come visit, and Gabe was back in my life after a twenty-four-year absence—my first love. Plus, Christmas was in a few days, and I was excited to give gifts to my friends and family. Something I hadn't put my heart into for years.

The doorbell rang. I grinned at the formality. Gabe was

welcome to walk in at any time, and he knew it. Hell, he'd just moved back out less than a month ago. Once the threat Sofia had represented was gone, he thought it would be best for our very new relationship if he went back home to his house.

I grabbed my coat and opened the door. "Ready," I said and smiled up at him.

He held out his arm, and I grabbed his elbow. He opened the car door for me, and I climbed in.

"Where to, oh gallant one?" I asked once he sat down and pulled on his seatbelt.

He smiled and winked at me. "It's a small town, Bridge, it's not like we have a lot of choices, but for you, nothing but the best."

"Pirate's Cove, then?"

"Right as usual!"

"Yay! I was in the mood for some dungies!" I said.

"I felt that," he laughed.

I narrowed my eyes and looked at his body language. "You played me!" I said. "You didn't plan anything."

"Not true, I planned on eating *somewhere* with you."

I slapped him lightly on the shoulder. "I guess it beats the 'Where should we go?' game."

"True. Just hint around that you are prepared, and let the lady accidentally choose. Works for me." His mischievous grin lit up the car or maybe just my heart.

We drove the twenty minutes or so to Garibaldi and actually found parking in the tiny lot next to the waterside restaurant. I loved it here. Gabe got us a table next to the windows, and although it was getting dark quickly, we enjoyed the last of the sun over Tillamook Bay. Dinner was nice, and the conversation and laughter was lovely, too.

When we returned to the house, I found that making

out in the car like a teenager was even better. Either I had to go in or invite him in, but we'd decided we wanted to take this slow. We'd both been burned by our exes and needed to do this right—*know* it was right.

So, I let him open the door for me and then kissed him some more against the car. Eventually, I made it through the door of my house after I waved goodbye to him.

Mr. Mittens greeted me at the door, meowed like a normal house cat, and rubbed against my legs.

"How was your evening, Mr. Mittens?" I asked as I bent to pet him.

Dull, at first, until there was an incursion.

"I thought we were done with those?" I asked, curiously.

You are still missing a piece of magic. They won't slow down until you have incorporated your last piece, he said. I vaguely remember him telling me something like this before. I guess I should pay more attention to the tidbits of info he deigned to throw me.

The house was dark, so Megan must have gone to bed. The only lights were the ones I'd covered the tree with. It was beautiful and peaceful. I'd placed a bench in the entryway for taking off and putting on shoes. I sat down on it and stared up at the glorious tree. Mr. Mittens jumped up and climbed in my lap, flopping over so I could scratch his belly.

His eyes closed, and his purr filled the space. This was peace and contentment.

"Tell me about the incursion?" I asked.

He continued to purr. *Nasty creature.* He paused. *Do you want the highlights, or the whole story?*

I looked down. I usually only wanted the highlights, which wasn't always fair. I'd discovered my cat had a flair for storytelling. Since I was comfortable and in a good mood I said, "The full story, please."

One periwinkle eye opened and gazed at me. *As you wish.*

I was doing my rounds. Checking out the boundary. Before you bought the original land back, I was pretty cramped here on just two hundred acres. I sometimes roam it all if I'm not needed here.

I scratched his head. "Sorry, my friend. I didn't know."

Hmpf. He gave his usual sound that meant a whole range of things and covered a bunch of emotions. He rolled to his side so I could scratch his ear.

I heard an owl call and flicked an ear at it. Was it the Lechuza I'd been hunting? It often took the shape of an owl.

I interrupted him again, and he sighed. "What's a Lechuza?"

I got an annoyed single eye look again, and another "hmpf."

If you listen, I will explain in the narrative, he said somewhat imperiously.

"OK, carry on."

I hid under some brush and watched. The owl glided silently past me, searching the ground. No, it was a regular old barn owl. I came out and started my patrol again.

He gave me a blue-eyed gaze to check if I were going to interrupt. I smiled and made the zip lips throw away key gesture.

A passing scent caught my attention. I sniffed; mouth open to catch more. Yes. The Lechuza was near. I drifted into the shadows, everything hidden but one eye. A massive owl, dark feathered and red eyed, fluttered down to the ground. It picked something up. I couldn't tell what she'd taken. I waited. The owl shifted into a woman, old and dressed all in dark clothing with long, dark, snarled hair. She put the object into a pocket and started to shift back. I leaped out and landed on the woman just as she completed her owl form.

"What happened to speak before you kill?" I interrupted him.

He huffed. *Some creatures are too dangerous. Now listen.*

"Ok, sorry, continue."

I crunched the bird's neck bones with my teeth, killing it, then to make sure it couldn't regenerate, I continued through until the head was severed. I picked up the head, carried it several yards away, dug a hole, and buried it. The Lechuza could not regenerate from that. I brought you back the body. I figured you might like to try owl.

He threw me a questioning glance. I had to suppress a shudder. It wasn't an owl; it was a shapeshifter! I'd attempt to cook an actual owl. I'd have to fake it and throw it out, so I didn't hurt his feelings. "Sure, thanks," I mumbled. "Uh, where is it?"

The usual spot, he said smugly.

So, back door. I always waited until he wasn't around to dispose of his "gifts."

"What did she put in her pocket? Did you check?" I asked.

I do not know. What use do I have for things I can't eat? he asked.

Well, that made sense. I mean he did have use for his bowls and apparently my bed. But he didn't have anywhere to put things or carry things about. I guess I could get him a fancy collar if he wished for something of his own.

"Do you want something of your own?" I asked. "I can find a space for you that would be just yours if you want something. I could get you a fancy collar or a special toy?"

Hmpf. I have the entire house to store items. I just have no need of things.

He was a cat; it only stood to reason he considered the house his. In a way, that made sense. He'd lived in it for close to a hundred and fifty years; it was more his than mine by that old tenant "possession is nine-tenths of the law."

"This is so gonna ruin your Christmas surprise," I said.

You got me a gift? he asked. His cranked his head back to look at me, and his eyes wide with surprise.

"Of course I did. You are my best friend. I love you, Mr. Mittens." I stroked his fur, and he purred louder.

Suddenly, he jumped up and ran towards the kitchen. I sighed. He probably sensed another incursion, and my peaceful night was over.

I stood up slowly and wandered to the tree. I should take the gifts I'd wrapped and throw them under it to give it more of a Christmas feel. I went to my closet and started pulling out gifts and placing them under the tree. It took a few trips, but eventually, I stood back to admire the bright packages and shiny bows. Even though the tree was undecorated, the gifts made the whole scene more festive. I sat back on the bench to admire it.

I heard Mr. Mittens making cat sounds as he trotted back in. He had something glinting in his mouth. He jumped up on the bench and dropped something in my lap.

This is for you—the Lechuza's item from her pocket. It's shiny; you might like it. His eyes glowed with excitement as he looked up at me. I had no idea where an owl hid its pockets, and I didn't ask. He probably shredded the whole thing, and I'd be sweeping up feathers for a week. I shook out the negative thoughts and determined I would love whatever shiny dirt covered item it was. I looked down at my lap and gasped.

It was dirty, but it was also a silver chain with little swirly charms hanging at regular intervals around it. It *had* to be!

I looked at my beloved cat. "Thank you Mr. Mittens, this is the best gift ever."

I picked up the chain and slipped it over my head. I let it

drop down inside my shirt, so it touched my skin. There was a little zing, a flash, and the necklace disappeared into my body.

Mr. Mittens sat down hard. *I didn't know what it was*, he said, surprised.

A cold breeze ran past me, and my hair whipped around my face for a few moments before it stopped. I felt complete. "You found it! The last splinter of my magic." I jumped up and gave a twirl. Then I picked him up and draped his limp body over my shoulder. We danced a few steps together. "You are the best cat that ever lived," I gushed.

I put him down when he started to wriggle. "Don't move, I want you to have your gift, too, even if you don't really need it."

I knelt under the tree and dug around for the large package I'd wrapped for him. I pulled it free and sat it down beside him.

What do I do with that? he asked.

"You open it."

He walked around, looking at the package. *I don't know how the item opens,* he said, confused.

I laughed. "You rip off the paper, it'll be fun."

He wiggled his butt and leapt into the middle, ripping and tearing into the paper with gusto. Frankly, that looked like more fun than the gift would be.

When he'd destroyed all the paper, I pulled the remainder off the gift.

What is it? he asked.

I picked it up and gave it a shake. "Come with me."

I walked into my bedroom and stood in the middle of the room next to the bed. "It's your very own, premium, memory foam bed."

I watched his reaction.

Really? Just for me?

"Yes, now choose where you want it to go," I said.

I should have guessed where that would be. I should have just chosen a spot on the floor. But it was Christmas, and it was his gift.

He jumped up. *Right here*, he said, his eyes glowing with excitement and happiness.

That's the whole story of how my lovely, king-sized bed gained a custom, memory foam, periwinkle blue, cat bed smack dab in the middle of it.

I sighed a little and looked indulgently at him as he rolled around in the new bed, relaxed, all four feet in the air.

Cats.

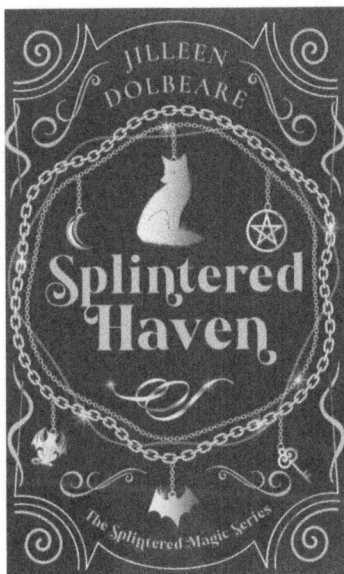

vinci-books.com/splinteredhaven

Brigid and Mr. Mittens thought they had earned their happily ever after but with the witches gone, the vampires are on the hunt.

As the dust settles from their previous battle, a new threat emerges. The power vacuum left by the witches' defeat has attracted ambitious supernatural entities, each vying for control of the magical realm. These newcomers aren't content with peaceful coexistence—and Brigid stands in their way.

Turn the page for a free preview...

Splintered Haven: Chapter One

"Megan, can't you get them to move faster?" I yelled. The rain had soaked through my hair, my jeans, and was running down my back.

"Maybe if you got me a horse, I'd be a proper cowgirl," she replied, waving her hands and running back to stop a cow from veering away from the gate.

"Have you ever ridden a horse?" I asked, huffing and puffing. I knew full well she hadn't.

"No, but you could teach me."

I was on the opposite side of our chosen five steers, trying to get them into the enclosure.

"I ride dressage. I don't know many dressage people who herd cattle on their off days."

"You loved going to those cutting shows," she replied.

"That doesn't mean I know how to herd cows! Now, push them this way." I waved my arms like a dumbass, yelling weird sounds at the small herd.

I looked back at Megan just in time to see her feet fly up and land flat on her back in the mud and shit.

I'm a terrible friend, because instead of running over to help her up, I burst out laughing. The double-up kind.

Once she got her breath back, she let out a string of curses that even a sailor would blush at. I pushed the last cow through the gate, closed it, and went to help her up.

"I'm just gonna die here. If I move, I'll be too grossed out to walk back to the house, just leave me to my cold, disgusting death," she muttered.

"No, you'll just have to gut it up. I still need help holding them while I shave them," I answered.

"Just shoot me." She gave a very dramatic moan. "I'm ready to go."

I laughed and offered her a hand. "No, you aren't. I'll hose you off when we get back, you'll live, cowgirl."

She reached out a hand. "Why are we doing this again? Don't we have people that can do this?"

"Uh, no. Jim is off tonight. We're doing this because our client doesn't like fur in his fangs." I pulled. We both slipped this time. I let go to catch my balance, and this time she fell forward into the muck.

"I'm getting a new best friend," she said after she picked herself up. She tried to wipe some of the muck off of her, but it made little difference.

She blinked at me, the sclera of her eyes very white in her mud covered face.

I couldn't stop laughing. She threw a handful of mud at me.

"Hey! I can't fight back, I have to keep this hand clean to use the clippers." I held out my right hand. It was only sort of muddy. I wiped it down my pants and held it out again.

She huffed out a breath of air. "Fine. Let's get this over

with. I need time to pack up and move to Australia. I'd be better off with the deadly snakes."

"Hilarious."

I opened the gate and closed it behind us.

"Which one do you want to shave first?" I asked Megan. I figured her sacrifice earned her first choice.

"That one." She pointed to a brown steer, standing docilely. "How do I hold it still?" she asked.

I hadn't thought that through. I wondered if I should have invested in cow halters, but it was too late now. "Um, just stand there so it won't veer away."

"Fine." She stood on the cow's left shoulder and I pulled out the clippers and shaved a foot wide spot near its large vein.

"That was easy," I said.

"Yeah, this won't be too bad," she agreed.

We went to the next one. It was also placid, and let us shave it without any issue. I relaxed.

The third cow wanted nothing to do with us. It bellowed, and charged Megan. She jumped out of the way. It ran to the corner of the enclosure.

"How many do we need to shave?" she asked. "I'm thinking two is great."

"I told him we'd have five cows ready," I said.

"What about the sheep? Sheep seem easier, and smaller. Lots smaller."

I sighed. "He said wool was the worst thing to get caught in your fangs. It takes forever to get out, and he wouldn't even hear of it even if I shaved them."

"Argh!" She threw up her hands. "Fine, let's go to the next one."

It took us three hours. Three. I was thinking of charging extra, but it was my fault for trying to be all inclusive and not asking up front for species or magical types. Now, I had to create a completely blacked out room and supply blood. Hopefully, he could chase his own cows down, now that they were shaved and returned to the pasture. I wasn't doing one more thing with cows—ever again.

When we got back to the house, we both needed to be hosed down. Megan was the worst, since she'd rolled in the muck, but I was barely better. While we'd chased cows in the corral, they managed to splash us with everything. I mean everything. I was covered in stuff I didn't want to think about. I hosed Megan off first, then she took pleasure in the repeat. It was ice cold, but we were already cold and wet. We stripped to our underwear on the porch, and I took our clothes directly to the laundry room and tossed them in the washer. Then we both headed to our respective showers.

Tomorrow was the grand opening of my B&B, so this was our last night of privacy. I was scared and excited. I was inviting strange magical beings into my house. I already knew I had a vampire, since he had special requirements. I didn't know what the others were. I was already regretting that choice, and considering changing it. Unfortunately, I was stuck with this group. I set my alarm for bright and early.

I'd set up a reception desk in the front foyer. It had a computer, and a machine for key cards, along with the main phone line. The first guest was checking in at noon, so I had time to go through the rooms for last minute inspections. My cleaning crew had done a great job, and everything looked amazing.

I'd even hired a cook for meals, and I could smell break-fast cooking. He'd started today. Megan had found him on one of the supernatural only sites she'd found and started advertising on. Megan said he was a shifter, but we didn't know what kind. That seemed invasive since he hadn't offered to tell us.

I rechecked the room we'd blacked out for the vampire. He'd been very specific in his needs, as I would be too if I were severely allergic to sunlight. At least on the Oregon coast, sunlight was a rare happening this time of year.

We had three other guest rooms that were being rented at the same time, three days for two of them and five days for the other two. I was nervous, excited, and scared to see how everything would go. I didn't need the money, but it would be glorious if the new business could support itself and pay my new staff.

After this week, I also had a couple of supernatural creatures coming to stay in the stables and hunt in my woods. We'd stocked cattle, sheep, and goats for easy access to food, and would allow deer or elk to be hunted in the woods. Mr. Mittens would supervise those hunts.

Since I had a dragon to feed, we needed to keep the prey levels up and at healthy numbers, although Mr. Mittens was currently teaching him to realm walk so he could hunt for himself on other worlds.

When I came down the stairs from checking on the rooms, Megan was on the phone.

"Yes, that is completely fine. We do allow small pets as long as they are in a carrier or on a leash when they aren't in your room. That's for their safety. We do not guarantee the safety of pets." There was a pause while she listened. "This is a private bed and breakfast, not a large chain, those are the rules." Another pause, I was close enough now to hear a tinny voice over Megan's headset. "That's fine. Have a good day."

"What's up?" I asked, curious.

"I think that was a human. I hope I discouraged her from making a reservation."

"If she calls back just say no vacancy."

She wrote something on her message pad. "Yeah, good idea," she answered, distracted.

"Was there something else?"

She looked up. "Huh? Uh, no. I was writing down some notes and ideas on what we can add to figure out guest species and requirements. If we just do a generic, 'dietary needs' that would cover things like blood." She snorted. "I'm not chasing cows again."

"Me either, but if I'd had earlier notice, we could have had Jim do it," I remarked.

"Yeah, that is why we are making this new checklist."

"Is Madison watching the desk tonight?" I asked.

Madison Whelan was one of the Whelan werewolves. They were friends and owned a local restoration and construction business. The Whelan's had begun the restoration and transformation of my old Victorian house. They'd quit after their father had been killed by witches. Madison hadn't been into the family business, and was still searching for her dream career. She filled in for them when they needed a receptionist on occasion, and had applied to work as a receptionist here when I was looking for one. She said she was interested in hospitality, and since she was a friend, and was Megan's boyfriend's sister, it had been a great fit for all of us.

Plus, it wasn't easy searching for supernatural workers for a supernatural B&B. It wasn't like we could put an ad on the general internet or in the local paper. Megan had started the process of advertising across the splinters, as Mr. Mittens called them. But, we hadn't gotten very far yet. Basically, just Faerie.

Just as I thought of him, Mr. Mittens wandered up and jumped up on the desk.

I'll have the duck tonight, he mindspoke to me.

I glanced at the clock. Was it feeding time already? "Oh?" I added a smile.

With cream, of course.

"Of course, your majesty."

He blinked his large periwinkle blue eyes at me, *Hmpf,* he said with disgust at my snark.

Mr. Mittens was a Splintercat. A cat-like creature from another world that could shapeshift, and realm walk. When he was here with me, he was a fluffy blue-mitted Ragdoll that was more than a little ridiculous, liked to sleep in the middle of my bed, and kept my woods clear of evil, dangerous creatures who were attracted to the power that a link to the Fae realm provided my land.

Since I'd finally re-integrated all of my magic, the loose power was less, but it hadn't stopped all of the incursions. Mr. Mittens had a little more time for me, but he still made his patrols, and discouraged or killed marauders.

He jumped down and headed to the kitchen, floofy tail swaying with his walk.

"Brigid!" Megan yelled.

"What?"

"Where did you go? I've been talking to you." She waved her hand in front of my face.

"Rude. I was just lost talking to Mr. Mittens and lost in thought, what did you say?" I asked.

"I said that Madison was on for the next three swings, then she'll do days for the next two."

"Oh, yeah, right. I forgot." I looked at my phone. We'd be having guests soon. I'd set check in at three in the afternoon, but since this was our first group of people, and everything was ready and set up, I'd allowed the first group ever to have early check in. People would be arriving at any moment.

I'd had our cook make up sandwiches for lunch just in case anyone was hungry, and he was going to do a celebratory supper. I wasn't going to offer three meals in general, but I thought I would for this first day. Then, he was on call for room service, or purchased meals for lunch or dinner. Breakfast was included.

I hurried and made Mr. Mitten's dinner, and rushed back out just in time to hear a car coming up the newly paved drive. My palms started to sweat. This was it!

"Here comes someone," I said to Megan, she nodded. She also looked excited and nervous. She stepped behind the desk. She was going to play receptionist, and I was playing hostess.

A couple stumbled through the door with their baggage. They looked like normal humans, but so did I. I greeted them, and directed them to the desk. Megan took their information and gave them their keys. We'd put them on the third floor.

"If you'll follow me, I'll show you the dining room and the elevator," I said and waved a hand for them to follow me. I stopped at the elevator on the other side of the massive staircase. "The dining room is here, I swept my hand to the door. "Or you can choose to eat in your room, just phone the kitchen with your order." This is the elevator. Turn left on your floor, thank you for staying at the Secret Haven Inn." After they entered the elevator and the door closed, I leaned against the wall and exhaled a sigh of relief.

Megan came around the staircase. We gave each other a fist bump. "We rocked that," she said. They'll never know they were the first guests ever!"

We welcomed our two other guest groups, the vampire would be arriving after dark. The Secret Haven Inn was officially in business.

Grab your copy...
vinci-books.com/splinteredhaven

About the Author

Jilleen Dolbeare writes urban fantasy and paranormal women's fiction. She loves stories with strong women, adventure, and humor, with a side helping of myth and folklore.

While living in the Arctic, she learned to keep her stakes sharp for the 67 days of night. She talks to the ravens that follow her when she takes long walks with her cats in their stroller, and she's learned how to keep the wolves at bay.

Jilleen lives with her husband and two hungry cats in Alaska where she also discovered her love and admiration of the Alaska Native peoples and their folklore.